operation:
BLACKFLAG

a novel

by
Richard J. Kendrick

operation: BLACKFLAG, a novel, 1st edition: September 2015

Published by Consolidated Breadheaters Publishing

Copyright © 2015 by Richard J. Kendrick

Cover Art copyright © Richard J. Kendrick

Version 1.b.20150824

Dedication

For the gang at work
Blue sky idea:
Regulatory compliance for mad scientists

Prologue

NEXT FRIDAY

"Abomination!" he wanted to scream while hoisting his pitchfork in the air. Swirls of black smoke would snake off the torches the townspeople carried and twist around him, called by his fury and indignation. But Walter Renford didn't own a pitchfork and he hadn't the slightest idea where he could get a torch in this day and age.

Instead, he sat on a bench in the park with his cane leaning between his legs, hands clasped, one over the other, atop the handle. This bench, *his bench*, had the best view of the old park fountain and the recently restored shopfronts across the street. It had the most comfortable shade, with just a hint of mid-day sun filtering through the leaves of the tree behind it, which was even more advanced in years than he was. The sweet scent of fresh cut grass tickled his nose.

Fred, another fixture of the city park, sat beside him, tossing popcorn to a flock of pigeons. They cooed appreciatively.

And ruining everything was that gleaming, metal monstrosity the city built, crouching right in the middle of his view. The sunlight glinted blindingly off the polished, twisted metal. Heat waves undulated above its surface. An 'art installation,' they'd called it. Those idiots wouldn't know art if it bit them in the ass.

Statues should be bronze. And they should be people. Or people on horseback.

Walter grimaced at the sculpture.

Possibly, a statue of a horse alone could be acceptable, if it was suitably statuesque. But definitely bronze. He'd told them as much in his scathing letter-to-the-editor.

Now that letter, *that letter* was a piece of art! He'd packed so much thoughtful and well reasoned instruction on just where they could shove their damnable 'installation' that it was a wonder no one spontaneously combusted from reading it. He nodded. Yes, indeed.

The pigeons scrambled after another few pieces of popcorn, and the whop-whop-whop of a helicopter some distance away layered with the swish of the traffic around the park.

"That takes me back," said Fred.

"Does it now?" said Walter automatically, still staring menacingly at the 'art.'

The helicopter noise grew louder.

"Haven't seen a wasp that big since I was a boy."

Walter glanced over at his friend, and then followed his gaze out to the sky above the shops across the street. A giant black and yellow insect hung heavily in the air, curving steadily toward the park. He blinked slowly. "You're right," he said after a moment. "They just don't grow 'em like that anymore."

"It's the fluoride." Fred threw another handful of popcorn to the pigeons, but they scattered in wary confusion. "In the water."

Walter arched an eyebrow.

Fred raised his voice over the increasing noise of the helicopter. "Keeps 'em from gettin' as big, see," he said.

The wasp dropped low over the park, and crashed down upon the sculpture. The helicopter noise ceased, replaced by the groan of the sculpture as it sagged and crumpled beneath a bug roughly as large as a van. The creature twitched its head side to side before lifting slowly back into the air with a deafening thump-thump-thump of its wings.

Walter and Fred watched it gain altitude and buzz off out over the buildings.

"You're sure it was a wasp?" said Walter.

"What's that?" said Fred, looking up from the pigeons that had flocked back to the abandoned popcorn.

"I mean, you're sure it wasn't a yellow jacket?"

"Oh, no," said Fred. "Couldn't a been a yellow jacket. They never got so big as that."

Walter nodded. "Fluoride, eh? I'd always wondered about that." He surveyed the twisted remains of the 'art installation' and smiled. He'd be writing another letter about this. Oh, yes. And this time, they'd print it!

Chapter 1

ONE WEEK EARLIER

Goodness, how he loved the days like today, when he could get away from the harsh fluorescent lights and stark white walls of the laboratory. Doctor Vladimir Zmeyansky inhaled a deep breath of the crisp country air and licked his lips. He smiled as he raised the tripod of his spotting scope. Standing out here, amongst the knee high grass, basking in the sun, tasting the subtle perfumes of the spring growth—had he chosen the wrong path all those years ago? Should he have become a naturalist, instead? Would he have enjoyed his time in the out-of-doors so much if he were just there to look and hike? Could he have merely observed and described, rather than hypothesized and manipulated? And then there was the matter of control.

Ha ha ha. Scientist humor.

Silly to speculate on the matter, really. Vladimir knew himself well enough to admit he was set in his ways. Consider just how much of a spectacle he must be right now. Tromping through the dirt in his polished leather dress shoes, past thorny vines and thistles that snatched at his slacks and long white lab coat. He busied his hands focusing the scope, partly so he wouldn't adjust his bowtie. Again.

The gentle hill on which he stood afforded him quite the panoramic view of the surrounding clearings, and he swept the scope slowly across the field below.

A small herd of deer high-stepped amongst the weeds, grazing lazily. The fluid and nonchalant way they dipped their long necks into the brush suggested a complacency that was only betrayed by the twitching and swiveling of their ears. Good; they hadn't noticed him watching.

He gasped when he spotted the fawn, a tiny bundle of awkwardness leaping amongst the comparatively tall grass. For just a moment, Vladimir let himself get carried away by the unbridled joy of the youngster prancing through the meadow, creating a ruckus that almost certainly annoyed some of the older deer. He sighed and smiled, then, without breaking eye contact, he waved his hand.

Behind him, a muted swishing and shuffling told him that his assistants were following his protocol—well, they had better be, at any rate—so he started the stopwatch ticking on his wrist.

Within a few seconds, half the herd had their heads up and ears quivering. The fawn continued to leap and play for another moment, before even it froze. Vladimir noticed the sudden absence of birdsong. He felt a lightheaded thrill and realized he'd been holding his breath, mesmerized by the tableau of the deer, stock still but humming with pent up energy.

They weren't actually humming. Or buzzing, for that matter. That was just observer's bias and his imagination at work. And anyway, it would probably be a bit more of a keening or a whine.

But look at them. So alert. So tense! Just ready to ... snap!

As one, the herd broke into a run.

Vladimir watched them scatter in panic, but he kept the scope trained on the little fawn.

The young deer leapt forward with the others, its shoulders rising high out of the grass with each push of its hind legs, but its springy gait lacked the precision and power of the larger deer. The gap between it and the others grew rapidly. Some obstacles hidden from view— a gopher hole or some dry brush, possibly—caught up in its legs and it stumbled. By the time its head popped up again, the fawn was completely isolated.

Vladimir grinned.

The small deer scrambled wildly toward a windbreak of eucalyptus trees, and Vladimir saw a haze of dust drifting in the fawn's wake. No, a veil sweeping across the entire field, *following* the deer, picking up speed. The swarm! Before the tiny animal could reach the trees, the cloud rolled over him.

Vladimir grimaced. Damn it all, the magnification on this scope was too weak. Maybe one of the cameras—

He stepped back just in time to see one of his assistants drop to his knees and vomit. Chumley, the incompetent bastard! He'd transfer his ass to that ridiculous armadillo project out in the wastelands of New Mexico for this! If anyone on his team was going to heave up their guts, they'd damn well better do it on their own time. Vladimir could only hope that *someone* had taken some decent pictures of the experiment.

He huffed and stopped the clock. Oh! He nodded at his watch appreciatively and his sneer melted back into a smile. As he fished in his pant pocket for his phone, he looked back out at the field. Even with his naked eye, he could see the fog of insects—so many more than anticipated—tumbling over the grass. Yes, this was why he worked so hard, put in so many long days. The thrill, the exhilaration, *the adrenaline!* His fingers shook as he dialed his phone.

"Mr. Ransom," said Vladimir, "it's Doctor Zmeyansky. You asked me to keep you apprised of the pheromone experiment. I hope you'll forgive me, but I was just too excited to send you an email. We absolutely smashed the projections, sir. The attraction rate, the efficiency, the aggression, it was a thing of beauty." Vladimir laughed. "Listen to me gushing like a schoolgirl. I'll send you the full report as soon as it's available. It's a proud day for the Ransom Research Corporation."

Chapter 2

SUNDAY

The quiet was shattered by a crashing klaxon.

Diane Jones moaned.

Her hand snaked out, the meat of her palm slapping down atop the alarm clock. Silence.

"Darryl," she said.

Early morning sunlight snuck through the slats of the window blinds, just barely illuminating the gentle rise and fall of the blanket beside Diane.

"Darryl!"

"Hmm," said the blanket.

"Wake up!"

The blanket made no reply and resumed its earlier rhythm.

The silence took on the palpable shape of an irritated squint. The blanket rippled violently and disgorged Darryl onto the floor with a thump.

"Geezus. Diane. What the hell—"

"If you'd just get up when I tell you—"

"It's Sunday morning. I can't believe this crap—"

"—we wouldn't have to go through this same damn thing—"

"—first thing in the morning. Kicked me right out of the damn bed—"

"—every morning. Some things need doing first thing in the morning—"

"—I get to sleep in on Sundays. Only day of the week I sleep in is Sunday."

"—and I can't count on you to do 'em," said Diane.

Darryl leaned against the bed and rubbed his face. "Why am I up, Diane?"

"You got to spray those wasp nests in the barn."

"It's Sunday morning—"

"Quit your whining and spray those nests," she said. "If you don't hurry up, it'll warm up and you won't get within ten feet of 'em."

Darryl slowly drew his knees up, then sighed loudly as he got to his feet. "It's Sunday," he muttered as he picked his way carefully around the bed, which occupied most of the space in the small room. "Only day I get to sleep in is Sunday." He shuffled through a pile of clothes, mostly by touch in the near darkness, and extracted some denim overalls. "Could have let me have my one morning," he mumbled as he stepped into the overalls. He snatched up a shirt and made his way to the door. He continued under his breath, raising the pitch of his voice, "Have to spray those wasp nests. Can't wait 'til tomorrow."

Darryl wrenched open the door, which scuffed the floor and stuck once partially open. "Least you could do is go start fixin' breakfast, if I have to be up first thing on a Sunday—" He tugged the door closed behind him, which creaked in protest before giving way and snapping shut.

Diane listened as Darryl stomped down the hallway. "And be sure to get 'em all!" she shouted just before Darryl was out of earshot. She settled back against her pillow, holding her breath as she listened for more footsteps.Then she snuggled up tight in the blanket and shut her eyes.

Darryl let the screen door slam behind him and rubbed the sleeves of his flannel shirt to fight off the crisp morning air. He stomped down the weathered wooden porch, and then crunched up the gravel path that lead from the farmhouse to the old barn.

Over the years, the sun had baked the building from its once typical barn red, to a dusty, rusty hue. The open hay loft, which at some indeterminate point in the past had stood squared and true, sagged noticeably. But as Darryl leaned back against the weight of the main door, it slid smoothly and almost silently on well oiled tracks.

"Get me up, first thing on a Sunday morning," he said as he trudged into the barn. He looked over a poorly organized collection of cans and plastic jugs—most covered with dust, a few crusted or corroding—stacked on a bowed wooden shelf on one wall. He craned his neck forward and selected the only clean and shiny can in the bunch. He squinted at the tiny print on the label, but the feeble light coming in through the open door was insufficient. He shrugged, grunted and tucked the can under one arm.

Beneath the shelves, and occupying a considerable portion of the available wall space, lay a battered metal ladder. Darryl heaved it with one arm, and steering it awkwardly a few feet above the ground, only banged it into a handful of obstacles as he exited the barn.

"That woman better have breakfast ready when I get back in there, if she knows what's best..." Darryl pointed the ladder up at the sky and hauled on a cable. The ladder clicked and kerchunked until it reached almost to the eaves of the upper story, and then Darryl eased it down to rest against the wall.

"Eggs *and* bacon *and* hashbrowns, if she knows what's best," he said as he climbed one rung at a time. He reached a satisfactory height and stopped to examine the can for an instant. Eh, too much to read. He shook it a few times for good measure and depressed the nozzle. "Hm," he said as a jet of bug spray arced from the canister. Darryl steered the stream onto a muddy lump of a wasp nest tucked under the eave. "*And* pancakes," he said.

Chapter 3

MONDAY

Doctor Stuart Rhys-Billingsly polished the laptop monitor with a cloth. Again. He blinked at it, his frown pulling his jowls into starker relief. Maybe there was some windex in the cupboard. He thoughtlessly pulled off his bifocals, giving the thick lenses the same treatment with the cloth while he contemplated the possibility of a trigger sprayer full of blue liquid. No, probably not. He reseated the glasses on his face.

"Ah," he said and chuckled. Nevermind, then. He squared the laptop with the edge of the lab table.

Stuart spared a glance around the room—suddenly much less *hazy and smudged,* dummy—to check that nothing was out of place. Mondays brought out the paranoid in him, and he scanned the space for evidence of janitorial tomfoolery that might have occurred over the weekend. Which wasn't at all fair. Not everyone was quite so detail oriented as he was. For instance, after he'd noticed that every light switch, outlet, jack, and ceiling light fixture—he'd had to climb up on a chair to see those properly—was individually numbered, he'd sort of accidentally memorized all of the numbers. Stuart was pretty sure the janitorial crew wasn't quite so compulsive. Which was a shame, really, but they must have their work cut out for them. Here at Ransom Research there must be dozens of labs—well, let's see, Stuart's lab was 227, which probably meant there were about— Stop it! He was getting sidetracked.

His eye landed on the big anatomical diagram of a wasp that he'd hung on the wall. *Vespula germanica,* by the look of it. Not his favorite species, but there weren't exactly a lot of wasp diagrams on the market. He'd flaunted protocol by putting that up—which always made him feel just a bit like a rebel, even though he'd done it with adhesive so it wouldn't leave a mark if someone made him take it down—but this was *his* lab, gosh darn it.

"Right," he said. "Get on with it." He stretched his fingers, and then tapped a few keys on the laptop with his self-taught three-finger technique.

He picked up a small plastic container fitted with a pump spray head and read the label. "Formula three-beta-twenty-four," he said, and typed that into the laptop. Not that he couldn't remember, of course. He'd only been thinking about formula three-beta-twenty-four during most waking moments for the last month. Well, he hadn't *precisely* been thinking about this formula. He'd been swimming in the data from its last two immediate predecessors. But he'd been searching for the key, the pattern that would show him what to tweak. The roadmap, as it were, that would lead to three-beta-twenty-four and finally hitting the benchmarks that Mr. Ransom had personally tasked him with. He'd mixed it and bottled it last Friday. Printed the label and affixed it himself. He knew what he was holding, but it didn't pay to make assumptions.

He turned his attention to the few dozen plastic boxes that covered the majority of the lab table. Each box was identical, clear plastic, with a fine mesh top, and a single wasp occupant. "Breathe deep, my little devils," he said, and sprayed one pump of mist from the bottle through the mesh of each box.

A career spent studying wasps had helped Stuart develop a subtle and nuanced insight into their moods and behaviors. He observed his specimens and noticed no immediate reaction to the new formulation. They were all in a baseline normal state, which is to say, completely enraged. His face twitched into a tiny smile.

With one possible exception. He furrowed his brow and tapped on the mesh of one of the boxes.

In a blink, the wasp in question flitted to the top of the container.

Stuart shot back—jostling the box, toppling his ~nd cradled his hand to his chest. "Son of a gun!"
᠁ from foot to foot, before finally

ιand beneath a cool stream of ink. First thing on a Monday /hat a delightful way to start the

Chapter 4

TUESDAY

Doctor Stuart Rhys-Billingsly inhaled sharply as he pressed the power key on his laptop, immediately regretting having thoughtlessly used his right hand to do so. Already, today was not shaping up to be an improvement on the day before. Contrary to the norm, his hand was worryingly swollen, burning an angry red, and quite sensitive to the touch.

As the screen lit up and the computer whirred to life, Stuart looked over the collection of wasps. "Good morning, three-beta-twenty-four group, you little bastards, how are we feeling today, hmm?" His eye drifted over to the box that contained his nemesis from yesterday. It wasn't properly squared up with the other ontainers, and now that he'd noticed it, it would eat m all day until he fixed it. Best to just nip that i d.

He reached, stopped, rolled his eyes, and then tried again with his uninjured hand. He tapped the lid, which slid clean off the container. "Crap," he said and yanked his hand back.

Stuart inched closer. How the heck was he going to get the lid back on without that little devil stinging him ag— "Oh, darn it," he muttered. No wasp. It must have escaped yesterday. His gaze shot to the ceiling and he flinched. Moving at a snail's pace and in a slight crouch, Stuart made his way to one corner of the room. He began a nervous, but methodical, search of the lab, floor to ceiling in an expanding radius. Not that he was entirely sure what he'd do once he found the little monster, but it turned out not to matter. The wasp was either gone or too well hidden to find. Hopefully it had escaped out an air vent or something. Fantasies that it was well hidden and, essentially, biding its time would have him looking over his shoulder all day. Gods, he did not need frayed nerves to go with the aching of his hand.

He returned to the laptop that was waiting so patiently for him and logged himself into the system. His experimental protocol didn't include 'escape' as one of the options. Sloppy—

He could feel it lurking just outside of his field of view—

No. Where was he? Right. Sloppy. Sloppy because it had happened or sloppy because he hadn't anticipated that it might happen, and included it in the protocol? He was going to have to think on—

Gods darn it, he was tensing up. Hunching his shoulders to protect himself against it, like that could work—

Focus, Stuart. It was the pain in his hand. That was making it so much harder to just ignore— Focus! Alright. The protocol included attrition. Statistically, it amounted to the same thing.

"Well," he said, wincing slightly as he worked the mouse, "not everyone's cut out for lab work, are we, fellahs?" He scrolled through the records on the computer until he realized he was leaning very close to the screen and squinting. He growled, suddenly pushed himself away from the laptop, and sidestepped to the wasp cages. His hands flew out, slammed the open lid back onto the empty box, and then teased it gently into line with the others.

He stepped back, breathing rapidly, closed his eyes and took a long deep breath. When he opened his eyes again, his shoulders had settled back and his face was slack and calm. The box remained empty, but the collection was neat and true and perfect. The prisoners were humming with a renewed fury. Stuart found this sound comforting.

He finished scrolling to the correct entry on the computer. Very gingerly, he clicked 'deceased.'

"Alright, the rest of you," he said. "Let's have a look at you, then." He tilted his head so he could properly see through his bifocals. "Well, you devils are looking plump, aren'tcha?"

Chapter 5

TUESDAY

"Mr. President—"

"Don't say it, General," said President Robert Goodson. "I already know what you're going to say." The president stood rod straight, shoulders back, and spoke assertively to a space slightly above and to the right of General Greffen. "'I've got bad news, Mr. President.'"

Greffen maintained his unreadable exterior. He'd cultivated it during a lifetime of service to his country and now it fit him like an old pair of jeans: comfortable, functional and unobtrusive. Of course, he came off as one note. Aloof, even. Predictable? Good. That meant no one saw the gears turning. His mirthless facade could certainly handle a gentle ribbing from the president, but truthfully, he really wasn't in a joking mood today.

President Goodson relaxed his shoulders, and shrank back from towering to merely tall. "I'm getting tired of Louise bringing me down here—" he gestured vaguely to the woman beside him and at the White House Situation Room, which was buzzing with stern and serious activity "—so you can say, 'I've got bad news, Mr. President.' Just once, I'd like to come down here and you can say, 'I don't have bad news, Mr. President.' We can have cake and punch in celebration of General Greffen *not* having bad news."

Could he tell Elizabeth about this when he got home tonight? If the story hadn't broken yet, then it was classified— Jesus, but it already *was* tonight. Which meant he'd be pulling an all-nighter. And if Elizabeth had already heard, she'd probably be pulling an all-nighter, too. He'd have to call her after this briefing.

Louise McCracken, White House Chief of Staff, cleared her throat. Her face hadn't so much as twitched during the President's monologue. Not that Greffen had ever seen her smile or laugh. "What have we got, General?" she said.

"Bad news, Mr. President," said General Greffen.

President Goodson sighed and folded his arms. "How bad?"

"A Red Cross camp in the African nation of Julala was attacked one hour ago. Five aid workers were killed in the attack, and the remaining twenty have been taken hostage."

The president's good humor disappeared, replaced by a steely seriousness and a hint of exhaustion. Or was Greffen just projecting?

"Do we know what they want, General?" said the president.

McCracken shot President Goodson a look. "Does it really matter what they want, Mr. President?"

"Three groups have claimed responsibility," said Greffen. "We're working now to determine who actually made the attack."

"Is there any chance we can rescue the hostages?"

"Until we know more, Mr. President, I really can't say."

The president looked Greffen square in the eye, and then his expression softened. "This one hits a little close to home, doesn't it, George?"

Greffen gave one quick nod.

"Does Elizabeth know?"

"I'm not sure."

"Well—" President Goodson straightened up and set his jaw "—keep me posted, General." He turned to leave.

"I will, sir. Have a good night, Mr. President."

Chapter 6

WEDNESDAY

Stuart wheezed from the effort of pushing his way through the door of his lab. He was no spring chicken, certainly, and hardly a marathon runner, but this was ridiculous.

The ghost of his reflection in the narrow door window caught his eye. Gods, he looked awful: skin ashen, eyes sunken. Why hadn't he glanced in a mirror before heading in this morning? One look at that and he'd have taken a sick day. His body was all but screaming at him that he needed it. And now that he'd noticed—but he was here already, might as well make the most of it.

The door brushed his hand as he entered and he winced. His hand was even puffier than the day before and quite alarmingly purple. He instinctively cradled it against his chest. Come to think of it, he'd been doing that all morning. Not that he was noticing much, what with this discomfort radiating up his arm to his shoulder, crowding out thoughts of pretty much anything else. He probably should have taken an ibuprofen, or something. Did he have any here? The data-entry screen appeared on his laptop. When the hell had he settled down and logged in? And what in the name of the gods was that humming?

Stuart's mouth dropped open, and he stood up so fast he felt woozy. Well, woozier. There should be buzzing, but he was hearing humming. There was no way the pitch should be so low. He snatched up his caliper with his injured hand with hardly a whimper and set to work recording the measurements of the wasps

They'd already grown to be easily as long as a finger.

"This can't be right," he said has he typed in the last of the numbers. He struck a few keys, and the computer drew a graph on the screen showing a steeply climbing curve.

"My gods," he said and staggered back from the laptop. He dashed in the direction of the door, knocking over a stool as he went, hardly daring to take his eyes from the screen. Stuart pulled the telephone handset from it's perch beside the door and dropped it. He scrambled to grab it as it bobbed on its springy cord. Finally grasping it, he wedged it against his ear and stabbed at several of the buttons on the phone.

"Mr. Ransom? It's Doctor Rhys-Billingsly, in the growth project? It's the three-beta-twenty-four group, sir," he said. "The wasps, sir. There's something wrong." Stuart paused, trying to tie his racing thoughts to coherent sentences. "We have to destroy them! They're—" He silently shaped a mouthful of words before finding his voice again. "—they're huge!"

Ransom replied, a squeaky chatter from the tinny telephone speaker almost inaudible over the dull drone of the wasps in the room, but Stuart was concentrating on the growth curve.

"There's no telling how big—" said Stuart, "—I mean, just imagine if one—" his brow knitted "—if one..." His nausea ratcheted up a notch and he licked his lips. "Sir, I'm afraid one of them has gotten out."

Chapter 7

WEDNESDAY

President Goodson reclined on the couch in the Oval Office, one arm stretched across the over-stuffed back, his legs crossed, and a manilla folder balanced on his lap. He stared at a typewritten page in the folder, but the words on the page were no longer coalescing into intelligible thoughts. The vice president sat opposite him, and the president could feel the man watching him. It made him want to fidget. To squirm. To jump up off the couch and pace about the room with a look of studious concentration on his face. Or he could stand behind his desk in an intimidating posture. Maybe leaning forward, with his hands on the desktop. Yes, that would be good. Totally inappropriate for the moment, of course, but if it meant he could stop pouring over this drivel—

A knock at the door interrupted his musings and he looked up.

His secretary stuck her head into the room. "Mr. President, your daughter is here," she said.

Oh, thank God. He nodded. "Thank you, Carol," he said as he closed the folder and stood.

Vice President William Rose took the cue and stood as well.

"I'm really sorry, William. We'll just have to reschedule."

"Of course, Mr. President. Thank you for your time." The vice president made his way to the exit, but stopped short when he reached the door, in order to let Jessica Goodson in. "Miss Goodson," he said, "what a pleasure to see you again."

Jessica hesitated just inside the Oval Office. "Good morning, Mr. Vice President." Her casual attire contrasted with the stuffy business formal of the two men in the room, but her posture and the glint in her blue eyes suggested an ownership of the place that made the president smile.

"And how are your studies going?"

Oh, for the love of all things holy, would the blowhard just leave already.

"Great, sir," she said. "I'm just finishing up finals week, and then it's spring break." She flashed him the same genuine, mischievous grin that the president saw in the mirror every morning.

"Is that right? Well, I hope you'll do something memorable with your time off. I know my college years were amongst the most enjoyable years of my life. And now, if you'll excuse me." He glanced sidelong at the president and then slid out the door.

"Morning, Daddy," said Jessica as she wandered properly into the room.

The president met her halfway, with just a little extra bounce in his step, saying, "Hello, Sweetheart. Walk with me for a bit. I've got to stir these stumps." He pushed open the door to the garden and they stepped out into the bright spring day.

"So what did you want to see me about, Daddy?" said his daughter as she sidled along beside him.

President Goodson had been looking forward to this for the last few days, but he was determined to savor the moment. The impish part of him, the stand-up comic from the campaign trail, piped in without a thought. "Here I send you to the best school, pay all the bills, hardly even interrupt your dates with strategically timed phone calls, and you jump straight to: What did you want to see me about, Daddy? No 'great presidenting lately, Daddy.' No 'didja save the world at all this week, Daddy?"

Jessica chuckled. "Did you save the world at all this week, Daddy?"

"Oh yes. It was pretty spectacular. But I hear they'll be casting Bruce Willis in my role for the movie. And I'm thinking, they couldn't find anyone with hair?"

Jessica laughed.

"So, you been working real hard?"

"Yes, Daddy."

"Doing all your homework?"

"Of cour—alright, the important bits. Yes."

"Staying out of trouble."

"You should know," she said with a smile. "I'm pretty sure you've got a spy satellite watching my every move."

President Goodson sighed and shook his head. "General Greffen won't let me. Something about misappropriation of military technology. I don't know. I stop listening to him when he gets like that."

Jessica laughed again, and he couldn't help but feel delighted.

"Ok, ok." He stopped, turning toward her at arm's length, with one hand resting lightly on her shoulder. "Let me have a proper look at you."

She mugged innocently while he put on a look of discerning scrutiny.

After a moment, he said, "It is this president's opinion that you've probably been a good girl. And if you ask me real nice, I think I just might let you borrow the plane this weekend. Maybe make a little jaunt out to California."

"What?"

He smiled.

"Wait, seriously? We're talking about Air Force One?"

The president beamed. "I heard a rumor that they're sending it out to the west coast for some routine maintenance on Saturday. Seemed pretty silly to send an empty plane back and forth, so I figured, what with it being spring break and all, maybe you and your sorority sisters would be interested in taking a little trip." He raised his eyebrows. "Hmm?"

There was that mischievous grin again. "So, Daddy," she said in a sing-song, "do you think that maybe the girls and I could borrow the plane this weekend?"

"Oh, alright. But bring it back with a full tank of gas."

Jessica squealed, loudly enough that the few secret service agents in sight turned to look.

One of them whispered into his microphone.

"Ooh, thank you, Daddy." She kissed him on the cheek and literally jumped for joy. For an instant, she was the little girl that always sprang to mind when he thought of his daughter. "California will be so awesome. Blue skies, the ocean—"

"We've got an ocean on this side of the world, too, you know."

Jessica waved the thought aside. "Theirs is better. Oh, and Mexican food!"

"Hey, we've got Mexican food— nevermind, now you're tempting me to tag along."

She shook her head. "I'll bring you some take-out."

"I don't know. Louise has been after me to take some time off."

Jessica gave him the 'ha-ha-not-funny' look that came stock standard with all teenage daughters.

"Anyway, I realize it's pretty short notice," he said. "I guess I didn't leave you a lot of time to pack."

She grinned again. Skullduggery. Shenanigans! "I can't pack yet," she said. "I need a whole new wardrobe."

"Your mother has taught you well."

"And a new bikini—"

"La-la-la," said the president, sticking his fingers in his ears. "I can't hear you."

Jessica kissed him on the cheek again. "Thank you, Daddy. You really are the greatest."

"Alright, go find your mother. I'll meet you all for lunch in the residence in just a sec." He stuffed his hands in his pockets and watched as his daughter skipped her way back inside the White House. A handsome secret service agent stepped away from a nearby wall and started to follow her, but the president gestured him over.

"How's the sorority life working out for you, Special Agent Franks?"

"It's a blessing and a curse, Mr. President," said Agent Desmond Franks.

The president chuckled. "I imagine it is. Take care of my little girl, now."

"Yes sir, Mr. President."

Chapter 8

WEDNESDAY

General Greffen sat stiffly in one of the high-backed chairs that surrounded the behemoth of a conference table in the White House Situation Room. The dark wood of the table reflected the myriad lights and glowing screens in its mirror finish, barren as it was save for the heap of papers in front of Greffen, and a couple tidy stacks by Louise McCracken.

A satellite photo of the aid camp in Julala topped Greffen's pile, and he stared at it intensely. But all he saw was the blood on his hand.

Not his blood. At least, he didn't think so. Scalpels weren't meant for combat. No guard between the grip and the blade. It could easily have slipped in his hand as he slashed it across the man's throat. Well, beggars can't be choosers. He shook his head and set the knife down gently on the desk beside him. His fingers trembled as he let it go.

"Are you all right?" he hissed, looking down at the body below him. A dark puddle slowly expanded away from the dead man. Greffen studied the grimy, asian face—mouth open in a silent scream, glassy eyes seeing nothing. "Elizabeth, are you all right?"

Thump. He glanced toward the desk.

Elizabeth's face crept into view, her nurse's cap crushed and skewed from bumping her head. They locked eyes, and she bit her lip. Finally, she nodded.

"Thank, God," he whispered. "Stay under there, and don't make a sound." He picked up the rifle that lay beside his attacker. Jesus, an M14. Greffen shook his head. Looted or sold by war profiteers? Shit, at least he knew how to use it. He checked the weapon and moved silently toward the door to the office.

He was supposed to be done with the killing. He was helping people here. This was a goddamn sanctuary, didn't they understand that?

How many more of them were out there? Were they hiding? Lying in wait? Or were they brazenly stalking from room to room? And just how many of his friends and colleagues would he be too late to save? He'd heard the pop-pop-pop—

Paper rustled and Greffen snapped his head around. The sight of McCracken thumbing through her notes knocked him sideways out of his memories. He took a deep breath and willed his heart to stop pounding. No sleep and too much coffee. He certainly wasn't a kid anymore, though he could have done without the daymare as a reminder, thanks all the same. He looked at the photo again, as if he could have missed something. "Olly olly oxen free," he mumbled.

McCracken looked up. "What did you say, General?"

"Hmm?" Greffen considered McCracken's stern expression. "Oh. My momma used to say, 'olly olly oxen free.' What about you, Louise? What did you say when you were a kid?"

McCracken squinted slightly at Greffen, effectively ratcheting the seriousness of her expression up a notch. After a moment, and with considerable gravitas, she said, "All-y all-y in come free, General."

Greffen nodded. "Come to think of it, I'm not sure the other kids said the same thing my momma said. But my momma always knew best, I think—"

A soldier appeared behind Greffen's shoulder. "Sir," he said as placed a document on the table in front of him.

The soldier hurried off as quickly as he'd arrived.

Greffen picked up the paper and scanned it rapidly. "Louise, we've identified the group responsible for the attack."

McCracken stood, her chair rolling back a few feet behind her. "I'll get the president."

Waving McCracken back down into the chair, he said, "No need to bring him down just yet. We still don't know where these bastards are."

McCracken leaned over the table, fists white-knuckled against the shiny tabletop. "Damn it. We've got to hit these guys hard, General."

His sentiments exactly! But Greffen shook his head. "We can't hit 'em if we don't know where they're hiding."

Chapter 9

WEDNESDAY

"He was so cute," said Mandy to her sorority sisters from her perch on the armrest of the couch. Her bare feet rested on the couch cushion, her toes poked under Celeste's thigh.

Celeste nodded her head and pulled a string of gum out of her mouth. "Mmhmm," she said.

Across from the couch, balancing on the too-small-for-two ottoman, Britney and Harmony gave Mandy their rapt attention.

"His hair was amazing," said Britney.

Celeste nodded some more and popped the gum back in her mouth. "Amazing."

Harmony pushed Britney playfully on the shoulder. "You didn't even see him," she said.

"Well, Mandy told me about his hair."

"I did," said Mandy.

"And I would have liked it if I'd seen it," said Britney. She folded her arms.

Mandy nodded enthusiastically. "She would have."

"'Cause he was so cute," said Celeste.

Court watched the gaggle of her sisters over the top of her paperback from the other side of the couch. Her glossy black thumbnail marked her place in her vampire novel *du jour*, as it had for the last five minutes since they had twittered into the common room and descended upon her couch.

What had she ever done to deserve this? Massacred a village in a past life, probably. Court read the next sentence. Again.

Harmony smiled and her gaze drifted to the horizon. "He was really hot."

Britney nudged Harmony, who caught herself before she fell off of their ottoman. "You didn't see him either," she said.

"Well, he *sounds* really hot," said Harmony.

Mandy chuckled. "And then his wingman showed up," she said.

"Oh, the wingman," said Celeste, a flighty smile on her face.

Harmony giggled. "He probably called himself that."

"He would, too," said Mandy

Court realized she was watching the girls again while unconsciously twirling her long black hair around her finger. She sighed quietly and untangled her finger. Thanks for this, Mother.

Britney chimed in. "What a nerd."

Harmony turned back to Britney. "Mandy told you?"

"Did she!" They all leaned in toward each other and giggled.

Court furrowed her brow and before she realized what she was doing, she said, "Wait. The blond guy had a nerdy wingman."

The girls all shifted minutely, and just like that, Court's corner of the couch was annexed into their ditzy world. Great move, Court. Why did she ever leave her room in the first place?

Mandy clarified, "No, the blond guy was the *first* time I went for a drink."

"Uh huh." Celeste nodded like it was just so obvious.

Britney added helpfully from the ottoman, "He was cute, too, though."

"Not as cute as the guy with the wingman," said Harmony to her ottoman-mate.

"Uh uh," Celeste agreed.

The front door clicked and swished open behind Court. She let her paperback flop closed on her hand and she looked over her shoulder.

The handsome, dark visage and exceedingly well-filled suit of Special Agent Desmond Franks appeared framed in the doorway. He scanned the room dispassionately.

Celeste's vacant bubbliness was suddenly replaced with keen-eyed hunger. She arched her back a little. "Hi, Desmond," she purred.

"Girls," said Desmond. His expression was friendly, but distant. He didn't let his gaze linger on the girls as he entered the room.

Court licked her lips when Desmond had looked away, and then colored when she realized she'd been so obvious. Her blush shone brightly on the cultivated paleness of her complexion. She hoped no one had noticed. *Why* had she come down here!

Jessica Goodson followed closely behind Desmond and swung the door closed behind her. "Hey girls," she said. "Courtney."

"Hey, Jess," said Court at the same time as the other girls greeted her.

"You all done studying?"

"On a break," said Court after the other girls finished 'yeah'ing and nodding. "I still have one more final tomorrow."

Jessica wandered in and dropped her bag beside an available chair halfway across the room. She sat on the armrest and crossed her leg over her knee. "I finished up this morning."

Courtney nodded. "The girls were just telling each other about the party they all went to together last night."

"Oh," said Jessica. She smirked.

If the other girls had any objection to Court's assessment, they didn't show it. Court mentally rolled her eyes at their cluelessness. At least Jess had half a brain. If Court had to suffer this banality entirely alone she'd scream. If Mother only understood the things she suffered for her damned sorority.

"This boy was *so* cute," said Mandy.

Celeste's predatory eyes continued to watch Desmond, but she managed a distracted, "Uh huh."

Jessica glanced around the room and then up the stairs. "Hey is everybody here?" she said.

"You're looking at us," said Mandy.

Jessica continued to gaze up the stairs, as though she could detect who was up there. "I mean, everybody else."

Harmony cocked her head to the side, looked up at the ceiling and started counting on her fingers. "I think Lisa and Lindsey are out."

Britney nodded beside her. "And Kelly has a final."

"Big Kelly?" said Jessica.

"No. Crazy Kelly."

Jessica brought her attention back to the girls in the room. With a shrug, she said, "Girls, I've got big news."

Court waited, her face impassive, unlike the expressions of airheaded wonder her sisters all shared. Finally, she said, "Well?"

Jessica grinned widely. "I met with Daddy this morning, and he's going to send us all to California."

"No way!" said Mandy

Jessica continued, "On Air Force One!"

Courtney didn't even try to follow the tittering and squealing that erupted from her sisters. When Jess met her eyes, she said, "Seriously?"

Jessica nodded, looking satisfied. "No joke."

Court used her well practiced, and now almost instinctual, blase attitude about everything to keep her expression stoic. Of course, she'd never admit it to anyone, but a private trip to California—in Air Force One, no less—was kind of cool. Not that there wouldn't still be trials to overcome. For instance, she'd be stuck in a plane with all of her sisters. And before that, she'd have to endure the inevitable—

Harmony's voice cut in over Court's internal monologue, "You know what this means, girls."

This time, Court rolled her eyes properly. "Here it comes," she said.

The girls all leaned in together, and in a register so high that Court was sure she'd suffered permanent hearing loss, they shrieked, "Bikini shopping!"

Court sighed. It couldn't have been a village. She must have wiped out an entire culture in that past life. "All of you have bikinis," she said. "Several, I expect."

As one, the girls adopted the patronizing look that Court saw all too often around here. "Really, Courtney," said Mandy.

"You can never have too many," added Harmony.

Britney continued, "And why pass up an opportunity to go shopping."

Celeste nodded earnestly. "Mmhmm."

Courtney put her head in her hand. Mother, you would have said precisely the same thing. And that's why her mother would never understand her. Yet, here was Court. A member of her mother's sorority, suffering the indignity of it all.

Jessica chuckled. "Count me in girls," she said.

Courtney sighed. "Fine," she said, loading the word with as much loathing as she could manage.

Jess smirked at Court. "And tell the other girls," she said, as if anything in the world could have stopped her sisters, anyway. "We leave Saturday."

Chapter 10

WEDNESDAY

Stuart sat on the floor of his lab, back against the wall, and eyes tight closed. He hugged his knees to his chest with his good arm while columns and columns of numbers flitted past his mind's eye.

There!

His eyes snapped open. He felt momentarily surprised to discover that all of his lab tables had grown to tower over his head. No, that wasn't right. He was sitting beneath them. When had that happened?

He shifted his body, intending to climb up off the floor, but his arm protested, and the room got wobbly for a moment. Something tapped him on the shoulder. He glanced over to discover the telephone handset dangling beside him. His call with Ransom. How long had he been sitting here?

He glanced automatically at his watch and started. Time to go home. No, wait, he'd worked it out. He had important things to do before he could leave. It was a conversion error. Order of magnitude. He pushed himself up, fighting through the light-headedness as he slid his back up the wall. He'd need to double check the actual numbers. Not just his memory. But he was certain. Decimal in the wrong darn place. Probably off by a hundred, maybe a thousand.

There was a droning in his head that practically vibrated down through his body. No, not all in his head. A droning in the room with him. He looked across the room at the wasps in their cages. Even from way over here, he could tell that they had grown. Order of magnitude. Could it be ten thousand times?

He had to destroy the subjects, before they got any bigger. Before it was too late.

He stumbled through the room on course to one of the cabinets, trailing his hand along the wall for support. He opened the cabinet, reached in and closed his hand around the cold metal of the spray can. It had made him sick to buy this thing and bring it in here. So undignified to use a common pesticide. Not that the devils appreciated anything he did for them. But the protocol demanded this contingency. Ooh, sprays up to twenty feet.

He turned himself around, trying to get the tiny print on the can to come into focus. Important to follow the directions—

"Hello, Stuart."

Stuart involuntarily clutched the bug spray to his chest, and then moaned a little when his arm protested. "D-Doctor Zmeyansky," he said.

"I'm glad I caught you before you left for the evening," said Doctor Vladimir Zmeyansky. He glided away from the door and glanced around the room, making a toothy smile at the specimen table that shifted into a sneer at Stuart's wasp poster on the wall. "I tried to call, but— oh, I see."

Stuart followed his gaze to the swaying telephone handset, lingering there for who knows how long, but when he looked back at Zmeyansky he caught the briefest of predatory grins that immediately dissolved. He tightened his grip, which drew his attention back to the insecticide. "Have to abort the experiment," he mumbled.

"But that's why I'm here, Stuart. You've been reassigned. I'll be completing this trial in your stead."

Stuart furrowed his brow, trying to wrangle his thoughts, which seemed unusually skittish and scattered. "Doesn't make sense— I designed— twenty-fourth— have to abort—" He held the can out in front of him, unconsciously aiming it at Zmeyansky.

"The decision's already been made," said Zmeyansky as he weaved smoothly up to Stuart. His arm suddenly uncoiled and clamped onto the spray can. "It's my project now— My goodness, Stuart, whatever has happened to your hand."

Stuart couldn't focus his woozy mind on so many sudden shifts. He staggered a little and mumbled, "Stung. Few days ago."

Zmeyansky licked his lips and smiled. "You simply must have someone look after that. Why, I'd drive you to the hospital myself if Mr. Ransom hadn't completely filled my dance card." He turned and stepped back to the phone on the wall, yanking the can from Stuart's feeble grasp as he went. He snatched up the handset with his free hand,toggled the hook and dialed the operator with the base of the canister. "Yes," he said into the phone, "Doctor Rhys-Billingsly is feeling ill and needs someone to escort him to the hospital. No, an ambulance won't be necessary, will it, Stuart? No, just a helping hand, I think." He grunted affirmatively into the phone and delicately replaced the handset.

"I— I won't go," said Stuart. "Have to destroy the subjects."

Zmeyansky undulated his way over to the specimen table. "Don't take it personally, Stuart. It's just an experiment." He tapped one of the plastic boxes with the pesticide bottle hard enough to knock it out of alignment with the others. Its dragonfly sized occupant battered itself furiously against the walls. "And anyway, you're in no fit shape to run this project at the moment. Go to the hospital, take care of yourself. Use some of your sick days. That's what they're for."

Stuart felt his conviction slipping. Zmeyansky was right. He didn't feel good. But wasn't there more work to do? Some numbers that needed checking? He gasped when a woman in a security uniform materialised at his side and gently guided him toward the door.

Chapter 11

THURSDAY

Diane Jones opened her eyes, but saw nothing. The muffled sound of a lawn mower filtered through the thick blanket scrunched around her head. She shifted it away from her eyes, and then squinted against the harshly glowing red numbers on the alarm clock. One a.m. Who on God's green earth would be mowing the lawn at one-fucking-a.m.? The nearest neighbor was a half mile down the road and not bat-shit crazy enough to run a damned lawn mower in the middle of the night. She thrust her elbow out to the side.

Something grunted.

"Darryl," she said, and thrust out her elbow again.

"Shit, Diane, I woke up the first goddamned time," said Darryl. "What the hell?"

"Shh!" she said. "Listen."

Nothing.

Darryl pulled back the cover a bit. "What do I hear, Diane?" said Darryl.

"Dammit, it stopped," she said. "Some lunatic was running a lawn mower."

"You're hearing things, Diane." He pulled the cover back over his head.

A sputter of sound, followed by some creaking and clattering, broke the nighttime silence.

"There. What was that?" said Diane.

Darryl mumbled, "jus' 'a wind. Go t' sleep."

Diane heard his breathing become deep and steady.

She glared at the alarm clock and another minute flitted by. There would be burnt toast for this. And maybe even runny eggs.

"Lawn mowers," said Darryl to himself as he stepped through the barn door. He rubbed his side gently. "Middle of the damned night and that woman—"

With the first light of day only just breaking, the barn gaped, cavernous, dark, and fraught with tripping hazards. He fumbled for the switch on the wall. The lights buzzed on loudly, several only half-illuminating in protest of the morning damp, but feebly lighting the open space. Darryl gave the bulbs a disapproving look.

"—hearing things, I swear." He made his way over to the shelves on the wall. "Probably not the end of it, though."

A skittering sound came from overhead and dust filtered down in the yellow-green light.

Darryl looked up at the ceiling. Damned cats. He glanced over the containers of chemicals on the shelf, spotted the one he was looking for, and braced himself to heft the five gallon jug off the wall. "Bet she'll ruin my breakfast, like it's my fault she's hearing things."

A series of heavy thumps from above startled Darryl and his grip slipped. "Shit!" His forearm banged into another bottle, and several bottles and cans tumbled off the shelf.

Big motherfucking cat. Too big to be a cat, actually. "Hey," he said. "Who's up there?" He cast about during the ensuing silence for something, anything with some heft to it. Just in case. His eyes landed on a pry-bar on another shelf.

"You best come on down here right now, then," he said. He stepped softly across the dusty concrete floor, suddenly aware of every sound he made. The pry-bar sang softly as he slipped it off the shelf.

Stupid. He shook his head and tried to ignore the angst that made him feel short of breath. Must just be a cat up there. The boys would have told him if they'd seen any drifters 'round, not that they ever got many of those anyway.

He looked up the ladder to the hayloft, but there were no lights up there. Flexing his grip on the pry-bar, he cautiously mounted the ladder. His weapon thumped a rung. His boot scuffed. The ladder creaked under his weight, as it always had before, but today the sound echoed in his head. By the time Darryl popped his head up into the loft, his heart was racing.

The light was too poor to see clearly, but there was definitely no one up there. Darryl exhaled a long breath. Knew it was just a damned cat.

He thumped the planks with the pry-bar. "Skat," he said. "Go on. Get outta here." Some scratching from the back of the space called Darryl's attention, but it was too dark to see what made the noise. And no animals, cat or otherwise, came darting out of the shadows.

He climbed the rest of the way into the loft. "Hell of a day this is shaping up to be," he muttered. Expecting the mystery animal to make a break at any moment, Darryl stomped his way toward the open window at the front of the hayloft.

And then he came upon a mudball, big as a man's head, plastered to the wall of the barn.

"What the shit is this?" he said. He stared at it for a moment, wondering why it seemed vaguely familiar, waiting for understanding to dawn on him. No ideas surfaced. He raised the pry-bar, intent on knocking the thing from the wall, but hesitated. A strange feeling tickled at the back of his mind, some unconscious sense, suggesting to Darryl that this unexpected mudball was alive. And, rather more importantly, that he absolutely should not go smacking it with a big metal bar.

Bzzt. One of the dim bulbs down below finally lit up. The subtle change in the light filtering into the loft made Darryl frown; why, this damned thing reminded him a lot of the wasp nests he'd dealt with last weekend. He was gonna need a lot bigger can of bug spray.

With a chainsaw-like roar, a beast, easily half his size, launched itself from the shadows and knocked Darryl off his feet. He looked up from his position flat on his back and saw a huge pair of shiny mandibles clamp down on the pry-bar in his hand.

Through sheer, mindless, body-spasming panic, Darryl somehow knocked the monster off of himself and scrambled blindly toward the edge of the loft. "Diane," he screamed as he slid past the ledge and somersaulted through the air.

As luck would have it, Darryl's flight ended in an open space on the concrete, rather than atop one of the various pointy or lumpy farm implements that occupied much of the ground floor. He lay stunned and breathless, mouthing, "Diane!" for a few heartbeats, and then sucked in a lungful of air. He twisted his body to get back up on his feet, but stumbled as a pain stabbed through his right leg.

Darryl glanced at his leg and saw that his foot was facing the wrong way, and then snapped his attention to the sudden motion on the ledge of the hayloft. An insectoid head goggled at him, antennae quivering. The pry-bar fell from its mandibles and clanged on the concrete slab below.

"Diane!" Darryl screamed. "Call the sheriff!"

With a brap and a vroom, the huge bug lifted lazily into the air, finally illuminated by the harsh glow of the fluorescent lights.

The sight of the glossy black and yellow carapace ricocheted off the rational part of his brain and shot straight to his lips. "Wasp," Darryl mouthed. After an eternity that lasted about two heartbeats, he understood the word he'd just tasted.

The monster descended at a leisurely pace, its dangling legs a nightmare of sharp angles, its mandibles gnashing at the air.

Darryl scrambled backward on his elbows, dragging his useless leg, unable to look away from the approaching horror. He banged into something on the floor, which rang out hollowly. He saw a can skittering away out of the corner of his eye.

The bug spray! He turned his body, his vision a kaleidoscope of shimmering spots from the burning pain in his leg, and he spotted the familiar spray can just an arm's length ahead.

A weight landed atop him with a sickening scratchy crunch, bringing with it a fresh wave of searing pain. He dared not look back, and desperately reached out for the spray. His hand slapped down just a hair's breadth short.

Darryl screamed, thrusting his body away from the bug with everything he had left. He slid in his coveralls which were pinned under the beast. His finger hit the smooth surface of the can, which slipped for an agonizing fraction of a second, and then caught under his grasp.

Yippee-kai-yay! Darryl twisted back toward the creature, articulating something more like, "YippEEEAAAARRRGH!"

He held the can in front of himself like a shield, locking eyes with the monster, and depressed the button.

The spray can spurted and hissed and then gurgled and fizzled. White foam dripped down off the nozzle and onto Darryl's face with a soft splat, split, splat. For an instant, everything stopped.

He screamed, "Di—"

Chapter 12

THURSDAY

Reid Ransom—adventurer, playboy, founder and CEO of Ransom Research Corporation, venture capital wunderkind—reclined in the plush leather chair behind his desk. His feet, currently clad in the hand tooled Italian leather hiking boots that would soon bear his name and be available for sale everywhere people with obscene amounts of money shopped, were propped up on his dark, polished hardwood desk.

A wide variety of rare big game watched over the man who had killed them from mountings on the wood paneled walls, their glass eyes shimmering with the false fire of life, reflections of the dancing flame in the ever so realistic holographic hearth on the wall.

This office, so starkly contrasting with the clinical and sterile labs in the rest of the building, represented Ransom's Safari Period. He was a showman, of course—he had to be to raise the sort of dollars he raised—and he'd wowed more than a few big money investors with the shock of suddenly stepping into a high-end turn-of-the-century hunting lodge. He reveled in the knowledge that he could have made the pith helmet the must have fashion accessory of the season, if he'd so desired.

Ransom waited patiently with his phone cradled to his ear, turning his attention from his tanned, muscular, recently waxed legs to the laptop on the desk. It had been ignored long enough now that the screensaver slideshow had clicked on. Ransom admired his beaming face, flanked by a couple of bikini clad supermodels. His smile had a few of those shiny starburst spots that he always imagined as the visual representation of a 'ting' sound. And that was no Photoshop job. The boys in the lab had figured out how to make teeth so sparkling white that *they actually sparkled*. He'd sell that one as a top-notch cosmetic dental treatment. Until the profits dropped off. Then he'd have them mix it into toothpaste. Probably worth a few odd billion.

The phone finally stopped piping some studio saxophonist's royalty-free jazz wet dream into his ear, and a man came on the other end.

"Bill? Reid Ransom here." He flashed his dazzling smile at the empty office. "It *has* been too long. After we get off here, I'll have my secretary set up a lunch. Listen, Bill, I know how much you appreciate a little outside the box thinking. We've had a couple of unexpected breakthroughs at the lab this week, and I thought you'd be just the man to leverage this unique opportunity."

Chapter 13

THURSDAY

General Greffen thumbed through the stack of printouts in front of him on the Situation Room table. It never ceased to amaze him how quickly a developing crisis turned into a ream of written reports. How many soldiers fought their battles against Word for Windows instead of the enemy? But he was sitting here, reading the sparse black-on-white pages. They didn't stink of fear. They didn't give off waves of jungle heat. They weren't spattered in sweat and blood. But he used them to put himself onto the battlefield, despite the fortress of bureaucracy that contained him. So was the work of the soldiers battling an inconvenient Windows Update really that much less important than the soldiers holding a gun on the front lines?

Windows Update! Oh, how he loathed that damned Windows Update. He'd always click 'Remind me later.' He'd choose 'four hours' from the stupid list thingy. But would it listen? No! Lies! Five minutes later and it would be kicking him off. And then fifteen minutes worth of rebooting.

Greffen shook his head and returned to skimming the report. Decades ago, when he had been hefting half-again his body weight in supplies, risking his own neck to protect others, some general had been stuck down here with a similar stack of pages. He had received and followed orders spawned by those piles of paper. Heaven help us, a typo in the wrong place might as well be an IED.

And what the hell was that damned ding-a-ling song?

A second later, a tinny voice sang over the quiet bustle of activity once again, "Ring-diddl-ling-diddl-lingy-dingy-ring."

"Who the hell's ringtone is that?!" snapped Greffen.

Behind him, a soldier cleared his throat and said, "Um, I think it's yours, sir."

Greffen frowned and fished his phone out of his jacket pocket. The screen was lit up, showing an incoming call, but there were too damned many buttons on this thing. And most of them had nothing to do with talking to somebody. What was this world coming to?

"Ring-diddl-ling-diddl-lingy-dingy-ring."

Greffen would be having words with his grandson about this.

He thrust the phone out beside him. "Answer this phone, soldier!"

"Sir, yes sir!" said the soldier, snapping to attention. He took the phone and said, "General Greffen's phone." After a moment, he continued, "And may I ask who's calling?" The soldier nodded, covered the mouthpiece with his hand and said, "General, it's a Doctor Stuart Rhys-Billingsly for you, sir."

"Really?! Give it here, man. Give it here." He retrieved his phone and held it to his ear. "Stuart?"

"Hi, George," said Rhys-Billingsly's voice, rather nasal and digitized, but nonetheless familiar.

"Well, it's been ages. It's great to hear from you."

A few muffled coughs came through the earpiece, and then, "It has been a while, hasn't it? Gosh, it's too easy to lose track of the time. Of course, you must be a lot busier than I am."

Greffen grunted. "They make me earn my keep around here. And how's your mother?"

"Just got back from a cruise."

"At her age? Well that's terrific."

"Yeah. They put her picture next to 'spry' in the dictionary."

They both chuckled.

Greffen leaned back in his chair. "You know, I can still remember those fantastic cookies she used to make when we were kids."

"Oh, she still bakes," said Rhys-Billingsly. "I'll ask her to send you a care package."

"I couldn't ask—"

"I'm sure she'd be thrilled to do it, George." Rhys-Billingsly hesitated for a moment, and then continued, "So, George, I didn't actually call just to catch up. I— Well, I kind of wanted to ask a favor."

Greffen furrowed his brow. "Sure, Stuart. What did you need?"

"I mean, I shouldn't really bother you with this. It's just—" His labored breathing came through the speaker for a second. "Well, there was kind of an accident at the lab the other day."

"Are you alright?" Greffen sat up straight.

"Oh, no, no—" Rhys-Billingsly coughed. "I mean, yes, I'm fine. But one of my experimental subjects escaped."

"I see."

"And I was kind of hoping that you could, you know, keep an ear to the ground?"

"Do you mean, you want me to try to find your missing subject, Stuart? Doesn't the laboratory have procedures in place for that sort of thing?"

"Oh, sure. Sure. It's just, well, I was hoping, as a favor to me—"

"Ok, ok. Have you changed up your specialty, or something? 'Cause you were doing entomological research—"

"No, no, that's right," said Rhys-Billingsly's scratchy voice.

"And so your escapee would be...?"

"A wasp."

Greffen treated Rhys-Billingsly to a full-belly laugh. "You really had me going there, Stuart." After a moment's silence on the line, he said, "Seriously?

Because that's kind of a very small needle in a very large haystack."

"I'm not so sure about that, George. So, uh, look. I know how this is going to sound, but I promise you I'm not crazy. I'm pretty sure that it's about the size of a car by now."

Greffen blinked slowly and frowned. "Did you say a car, Stuart?"

"Yeah. Well, I mean, probably not a big car. More like a subcompact. You know, a Fiat or a Mini or something. Anyway, George, if you wouldn't mind keeping an ear open? Well, I've used up enough of your time. And I'll ask mom about those cookies. I'll talk to you soon, George."

The line went dead and the phone beeped in Greffen's ear. He set it on the table and stared at it until the screen winked off.

"Beretta," shouted Greffen. He kept his eyes on the phone, but he focused on the image of a young boy who, despite having had a much different idea about the way to use a magnifying glass and a bug together, became his fast friend what seemed like a lifetime ago. Someone stopped behind his chair, and he shook himself free of the memory and spun the chair around.

Colonel Camille Beretta stood at ease beside him. "Yes, General?" she said.

She looked like she belonged here, just another military staffer. Pleasing to the eyes of the predominantly male leadership, with her petite figure, and the girlish way she'd braided her long blond hair and draped it over her shoulder. But that wasn't why Greffen assigned her here. He knew that her talents were being wasted by shuffling paper at the White House. He just didn't like having an asset like her too far away.

"Beretta, my momma always told me to watch out for my friends."

"Yes, sir."

"And I'd reckon that she'd be right to tear me a new one if a friend asked me for help, and I didn't do anything about it." He met her flinty gaze. "Colonel, I want you to keep your eye out for any reports of a giant wasp."

The look of confusion that flickered across her face was gone so fast that Greffen almost missed it entirely. No, he certainly wouldn't let an asset like *that* end up under someone else's command.

"And keep it quiet."

Beretta smiled. "Of course, sir."

"Dismissed." Greffen leaned back in his chair, his eyes glazing over again. Just how big of a magnifying glass would we be talking? And who would manufacture a lense like that? Well, but someone has to make them for those giant observatory telescopes, right? So, really, it shouldn't be all that difficult to get something made. But it would weigh a ton. Tons, more likely. And then the bug would need to hold really still while he got it into position. He remembered having to turn and twist the magnifying glass just right, to get that beam of light to tighten up like the point of a pin. And then he'd get those spots on his vision, because it was so bright. Burning every damned thing, like a little pyromaniac. Children are evil. And then the mild mannered one grows up and unleashes a giant wasp—

"What have we got, General?"

"Strangest damned thing," Greffen mumbled.

"What's that, General?"

Greffen turned toward the voice and startled to see President Goodson and Louise McCracken across the table. He jumped to his feet. "Excuse me, Mr. President." He busied his hands shuffling the pile of reports on the table back into a neat stack. "We've found some of the hostages, sir."

"Just some, General?" said McCracken.

"I'm afraid so. Our intelligence suggests that they've split them up into at least two groups. We know that they're holding some of the hostages in a house just outside the Julala capitol city." He nodded at one of the nearby aids, who pulled up a map on the big screen. "But we don't know how many are there, or what they've done with the rest."

McCracken crossed her arms while staring at the map. "Do we have a plan in place for the extraction?"

"My people are working on one right now."

The President nodded. "Good."

"Mr. President," continued Greffen, "you should know that if we make a move on the house, the terrorists are likely to kill the other hostages."

President Goodson sighed and sat heavily in one of the conference table chairs. "What do they want?" he said quietly.

McCracken immediately snapped, "We don't negotiate—"

"General?"

Greffen sat back down in his chair, clasping his hands and resting them atop the pile of reports. "It's all the usual impossibilities, Mr. President. Release of political prisoners, removal of the current president of Julala, eviction of US interests, amongst other things."

"And can you find the other hostages?"

"We're trying, sir."

McCracken gripped the tall back of one of the chairs. "Take what you can get, Mr. President. The longer we wait, the bigger the gamble."

President Goodson frowned and looked intensely at the tabletop. "Be ready, General. But for now, we wait. Find me the rest of those hostages."

Chapter 14

THURSDAY

"As you can see, Mr. Ransom," said Doctor Vladimir Zmeyansky, "I keep all of the synthetic insect pheromone samples in this refrigerator in my lab. And they're labelled, of course." He turned one of the plastic bottles and indicated with a finger. "This one, for instance, is the wasp pheromone. It just wouldn't do to have these things getting mixed up."

Reid Ransom leaned back on one of the lab tables, elbows supporting him. His casual shorts-and-polo attire were utterly alien to Vladimir's lab. If Ransom weren't his employer, and if Vladimir had had any doubts about just how sharp the man was, he might have been offended. 'Casz,' as he was certain Ransom would say, was just not in his fashion repertoire. And for that matter, for his assistants at least, casual Friday was something that happened to other people.

"Absolutely right," said Ransom. He flashed a blinding smile, and Vladimir squinted a little against the glare. "So, Mr. Black," he said to the stranger that had accompanied him, "do the lab practices here meet your expectations?"

The man, dressed in a suit and trenchcoat of eponymous color, nodded, but remained as taciturn as he'd been during the entire tour. Vladimir didn't recognize him, but the close cropped hair and round rimmed spectacles triggered a sense of deja vu. It was almost like the man had stepped out of every spy thriller Vladimir had ever seen.

"Excellent," continued Ransom. "I told you Vlad was as good as they came."

Vladimir shaped his mouth into a thin-lipped smile. "Thank you, Mr. Ransom, for the kind words. And how rude of me not to inquire about your interest in the lab, Mr. Black. What brings you to us, today?"

Mr. Black studied Vladimir's face intensely, but said nothing.

Ransom pushed himself up off the table, and stuck his hands into his pockets. He projected such a sense of ease that Vladimir actually felt himself relaxing a little. "Mr. Black represents a group of researchers who will be independently verifying some of our project work."

"A vital aspect of our community," said Vladimir. "I wonder if you represent anyone I know?"

"They're all top men," said Ransom. "I'm sure we can loop you in on their progress once things are under way." He turned toward the laboratory door, but hesitated. "You know, Vlad, as long as we've got you cornered, we may as well pick your brain. You can still spare a moment?"

"Of course, sir."

"Terrific. Mr. Black had a particular interest in your pheromone project."

Vladimir licked his lips and grinned at Mr. Black. "Really? I'm particularly proud of that one, as Mr. Ransom knows."

Mr. Black remained completely inscrutable, which could have perturbed Vladimir, skilled as he was at reading between the lines. He'd made a career of it here at Ransom Research Corporation, after all. But he had an inkling that they'd arrived at the heart of the matter now. And reading the signals that Reid Ransom sent was really the important part of this meeting. Not that he needed to be goaded into talking about his pheromone research. He *was* particularly proud of that project; *that* was no lie.

Vladimir rubbed his hands together. "I've quite enjoyed the challenge of the pheromone project. It's a rather—" He sought the right word. "—fiddly topic. You see, the species will only react to a very particular compound. Sometimes it doesn't even extend to the entire genus. You can imagine my frustration when we saw encouraging results with *Vespula germanica*, and then a sixty percent decline in the response rate from *Vespula pensylvanica*." He shook his head and laughed. "Fortunately, we've ironed out that little wrinkle. And, of course, what works for the wasp has virtually no effect on the Africanized killer bee. The chemical structure of the pheromone for the scorpion is utterly unlike that for the brown recluse spider. Very narrowly targeted. And yet, once we've isolated and synthesized the active compound for a particular species, we can get a strong reaction from them with aerosolized samples in the low parts per billion."

Ransom chuckled. "Once you get the scientist talking, eh, Mr. Black? Don't forget your audience, Vlad. We haven't got the same stack of phDs that you do."

"Would you like the elevator pitch, as you call it?"

"Now you're talking my language—you see why I love this guy," Ransom said to Mr. Black. He gestured for Vladimir to continue.

Vladimir took a moment to organize his thoughts, to drill down to the really salient points that his employer—no, *Mr. Black*—would be most interested to hear. Don't forget the audience. And remember who was interested in the project, in case he had to recount the conversation later on. "Well, Mr. Black, it's like this: the pheromone only works on one bug. That exact species, however, can detect even the most minute, otherwise virtually undetectable, quantity of the chemical. A little bit goes a very long way. And when they sense it, they find it to be just irresistibly attractive."

"Fascinating, Vlad. Fascinating. And I can see you've really captured Mr. Black's imagination now. Looks to me like he's really chomping at the bit to get started."

Mr. Black shared a silent look with Ransom, and then stepped past Vladimir to the fridge. With one smooth motion, he retrieved the bottle of wasp pheromone and deposited it in the deep pocket of his trenchcoat. Then he turned and strode out of the room without a second glance.

"Not a man to mince words, is he?" said Ransom. He clapped a hand on Vladimir's shoulder. "Thanks so much for taking out some time for us today, Vlad."

"No problem at all, sir."

"I'll be sure to loop you into any updates from the new team."

"I appreciate that, Mr. Ransom." He smiled and licked his lips. "I'd be most interested in any pictures..."

"I'll see what I can do." He gave Vladimir's shoulder a firm squeeze and made his way to the door. With one foot over the threshold, he turned back. "Vlad, any idea what we should do with this stuff?"

Vladimir shrugged. "Oh, I haven't the foggiest. Marketing's really not my area. But I'm sure you'll think of something that'll turn a profit."

Chapter 15

THURSDAY

Court adjusted her bust in the pin-up style bikini halter top. Under the nasty fluorescent lights in the changing room, her skin appeared greenish beside the black and white polka-dotted fabric. She stared down at the cleavage that a few minutes of lifting, tugging, and re-re-retying straps had achieved. Not that she cared, or anything, about this stupid bikini. But Jess and the girls had *dragged* her here, and it *so* wasn't worth the battle if she tried to escape without buying anything.

At least mother wouldn't mind paying for this. She'd be so pleased that Court would be out getting some sun. Maybe there'd be a freak storm in California. Her lips twitched in a little smile.

Court glanced over her shoulder at the mirror behind her, taking in the view of the back of the boyshorts again. An awful lot of milky-white cheek remained uncovered, which was completely ridiculous. She sniffed and ignored the anxious thrill in the pit of her stomach, but smirked as an idea struck her. After pulling her phone from her nearby purse, she quickly tweeted, "Are we all just flesh in this meat market called life?"

She tossed her phone back into her purse, and threw a translucent black cover-up over her shoulders. It almost but did not quite cover any of those peeking cheeks. She nodded in satisfaction and then quickly changed out of the bikini, before she could waver and chicken out.

Once out of the changing room, Court glanced over the tops of the racks on the boutique floor. The store was empty save for her sisters, keen-eyed Desmond, and an impatient middle-aged woman with a fake smile behind the register. Court chose a path that would take her past Jess, weaving her way through the racks toward the register. She held the hangers in one hand and the bikini and cover-up in her other fist. Not that she was hiding it, or anything. And anyway, she just knew the girls were paying attention when she picked it off the rack.

"Oh!" said Mandy, causing Court to flinch just a little. "This is the one. It has to be this one." Mandy waved something above her head that was considerably more hanger than garment.

Britney leaned over from her place at the next rack. "Oooh," she said.

Jessica laughed. "I'm not certain, but I think they probably have public indecency laws in California, too," she said.

"So long as you aren't sure, we're fine," Mandy called back. She continued to rifle through the rack, but hung onto her selection.

Court hesitated as she reached Jess and, injecting as much sarcasm as any one utterance could handle, said, "Thanks *so much* for bringing me along, Jess. I *really* appreciate it."

Jessica gave a big belly laugh as Court continued on to the register.

Harmony, standing at the next rack over, held a hanger aloft and jiggled a sparkly swatch of fabric. "What do you think, Jessy? Will this one work your figure, or what?"

Jessica glanced up, and then continued her search. "If my dad sees me in that, there'll be hell to pay," she said.

"You'll be in California; when would he see it?" Britney gave the bikini a little closer inspection.

"There'll be pictures."

Britney waved her free hand dismissively. "Well, you could just not show him those—"

"No, I mean—" Jessica stopped shuffling through the merchandise, looked over at Britney and pointed, "—if I wear *that*, every tabloid in the world will have a photo of me."

Britney sighed. "Some girls have all the luck," she said. She made to put the bikini back on the rack, but paused and tucked it under her arm instead.

Transaction completed, Court tucked her wallet back into her lacy little purse, leaving a measured bit of the heavy steel chain that tethered the two dangling. It chinked against the counter as she accepted the ever so petite bag from the store clerk. She turned and leaned against the counter to wait for her sisters when Celeste slinked, yes, *slinked*, out beside Desmond.

"Hey, Desmond," she said in a husky voice. "What do you think, the blue or the red?"

Desmond kept his watchful gaze on the storefront. "They're both great, Miss," he said.

"You didn't even look!" said Celeste, stomping theatrically and making pouty lips.

Court rolled her eyes.

Desmond sighed and spared a glance for Celeste. "The blue one," he said after a moment.

"See, now, was that so hard?" replied Celeste, revving up her sexy voice again and underlining 'hard' with a flick of her eyes below Desmond's belt. "I'll go try it on." She turned and slowly made her way back to the changing room, swaying her hips with great exaggeration.

Mystery solved. *That* was why Celeste had insisted on wearing her tiniest miniskirt and four-inch heels, despite the chill spring air. She hadn't even worn stockings to stave off the cold, like any sensible person would do. Amazing the level of discomfort some people would endure for the sake of fashion. Court glanced down and brushed off a light colored thread that clung to her fishnets just below the hem of her pleated miniskirt.

"You gotta hand it to her," said Harmony after Celeste disappeared into the changing room. "She's not shy."

Hardly a moment later, Celeste called out, "Desmond, you couldn't help me with this for a sec, could you?"

Court covered her face with her hand and shook her head. Did she *realize* how ridiculous, not to mention pointless—

Desmond called out flatly, "I'm fairly certain I couldn't, Miss."

Jess laughed, and the other girls giggled.

"Don't worry about it, Desmond," said Jessica. "She's just trying to get a rise out of you."

Mandy guffawed. "You've got that right!"

Desmond shot Jessica a look that all too clearly said, "Really?"

Jessica laughed earnestly.

Court tried to shut off her imagination before anything involving Desmond and rising came to mind, but wasn't fast enough. Her cheeks suddenly felt hot. She must be blushing. Why didn't she just get a neon sign that said, 'fantasizing about the super hot guy.' Stop it, stop it, *stop it!* Gawd, she was making it worse.

The woman behind Court sighed and looked at her watch in a not so subtle way.

As if she wasn't on commision or something. Please! And it wasn't like she had to tolerate this madness *all day long*, like Court did.

Why hadn't she brought her novel? She should have figured that Jess's quick shopping trip would be anything but. Court sighed, pulled out her phone, and tweeted, "Sunblocked by earth, your tanlines now worm-food; do you lament an eternity lost to bikini shopping?"

Chapter 16

Friday

Colonel Beretta stepped out of the big, black Crown Vic. The short drive up the gravel road to the Jones's house had covered the thing with a layer of dust, and she couldn't help but wonder at the Army's wisdom of keeping a fleet of black vehicles. She extracted her dress uniform jacket from the back seat, pulling it on and fastening a button.

She hated this drab, dowdy uniform, with its calf-length skirt forcing her to take petite little steps, always threatening to trip her up. She'd had it altered, of course. Paired it with some shoes with at least a subtle lift to the heel. But there just wasn't much that could be done to drag this thing out of the nineteen-fifties, where it belonged. And if it weren't for her green beret, someone would mistake her for a member of the damned typing pool.

As she strutted up the front walk to the house, she remembered the last time some numbnuts had said, "Be a doll and grab us a coffee, sweetheart." She smirked. When all was settled with that, she'd had him busted down a rank. And he was damn lucky that was the only thing she busted.

Beretta's smile faded once she got a good look at the twisted metal of the screen door and the couple of splintered holes blasted through the wooden door beneath. Someone had hastily patched them with newspaper. Obviously, this was the right place. She knocked on the door, careful not to get snagged or impaled, causing it to rattle in the frame.

After a few minutes, and just as she'd decided to hammer on the thing, threat of tetanus be damned, she heard footfalls inside.

The door clicked open and a middle-aged woman's face, eyes bloodshot, appeared in the gap. "What you want?" she said.

"Mrs. Jones?" Beretta accepted the few seconds of silence as confirmation. "My name is Colonel Camille Beretta of the United States Army. I was hoping we could talk."

"No one here's lookin' to join up," said Diane Jones.

The instinct to show sympathy for this woman rose up, but Beretta squashed it. Diane looked like a tough woman, and her voice had an edge to it. Whatever she was feeling, she sure as hell wasn't going to tolerate some stranger's pity. "Ma'am, I'm here about—"

Diane sighed. "I know why you're here." Her face disappeared, and the door drifted open a few more inches as she trudged away. "Well, come on in," she said after a moment, "before I change my mind."

The screen door pinged as Beretta opened it and then snapped shut with a clang once she stepped inside. She glanced around the room, quickly taking in the worn wooden floors, the shabby furniture, the untold layers of white paint on the walls and cabinets that masked the crisp edges that must lay somewhere underneath. She pushed the door closed and followed Diane into the tiny kitchen. It looked like it was last updated sometime in the fifties, including the bakelite percolator currently burbling on the counter.

"Coffee?" said Diane. She opened a cupboard and pulled out a couple of mugs without waiting for an answer.

"Thank you, ma'am. That would be nice," said Beretta.

"Sheriff thought I was nuts when he got here." She poured some sludge into the two mugs and handed one to Beretta. "'Course, I must have fairly sounded like a lunatic, blastin' holes in my house, hollerin' about a giant—" She stopped and stared at the drapes over the kitchen window. "But he went out to the barn, and when he came back, he took down my statement without that smile behind his eyes. Looked like he'd been sick."

Beretta swallowed a mouthful of coffee. She'd had plenty worse. "Would you mind walking me through the events of that morning, ma'am?"

Diane turned around and fixed Beretta with a challenging glare. "It happened just like I told the Sheriff, and he wrote it down."

"Yes, he did, ma'am. I read it. But if you wouldn't mind?"

Diane sighed and folded her arms, leaving her steaming mug beside her as she leaned back on the counter. "My Darryl is a contrary man. Doesn't do a damned thing without my foot in his backside. I'd been after him all season to spray those damn nests. Kicked him outta bed Sunday last to make him do it. If the man had done as he was told, maybe—" She shook her head.

"Ma'am?"

"Right. Yesterday. Darryl was up startin' the morning chores, grumblin' about everything, as usual. I was here in the kitchen, doin' breakfast. And then he starts hollerin', which ain't usual. By the time I got out the door to see what the hell he was on about, he's screamin' about callin' the sheriff. I got up to the barn, and—" She stopped and closed her eyes.

"What did you see, ma'am?"

"I wasn't rightly sure. It was dark in the barn, and I was a ways off when I saw it. But it was big. Bigger than a dog. Shiny. Too many legs. Huge wings on its back." She took a shaky breath. "Darryl was underneath it. And it looked at me. And I ran.

"It chased me. Sounded like a— a damn riding mower, or a mulcher. Loud. I barely made it into the house before it caught up." She nodded toward the front door. "I gave it both barrels from the shotgun. Heard it leave. Called the sheriff." Diane turned her back on

Beretta again. Voice wavering, she said, "I was too scared to go back out there." She took a few deep breaths. "And then once the sheriff was here, he wouldn't let me go see. He said he'd never forgive himself if he let me see that."

"Did you hit it? With the shotgun?"

She shook her head. "Don't think so."

Beretta set her mug on the kitchen table beside her. "What was it, ma'am? What was it that chased you?"

"A wasp. A fuckin' enormous wasp."

Chapter 17

FRIDAY

General Greffen drummed his fingers on the table, staring at the cover page of the operations plan. He chewed on his lip and shook his head. Look, he understood the stress and pressure of the situation. These people needed to blow off a little steam when they could. And they probably figured there was no harm in it.

The plan was solid. He couldn't fault them there. If it hadn't been solid, he'd have sent it back in a heartbeat. But, in Greffen's opinion, the probability of success was high. And he hadn't got to where he was by being wrong about these things.

But Jesus H. Christ, it just wasn't professional! And to say that it was politically tone deaf. Shit, the least they could have done was be more subtle about it— No. No, that would be worse. Then some junior so-and-so would miss the joke entirely, pass it along to the press, and he'd never hear the end of it.

Greffen sighed. This was not the kind of shit he needed right now. And he didn't have the time to fix it, not with the president due at any minute. He'd have to try and change it later, and hope no one was dumb enough to leak it before all the references could be changed. If they even found them all, God help them. It's not as though an operation like this happened in a vacuum. How many different documents would refer— hell, how many different government agencies were going to end up referencing this operation in how many reams of paperwork. Maybe he really *should* try to nip this in the bud right now.

Goddammit, was he going to have fire someone over the fucking operation na—

The situation room door opened and President Goodson and Louise McCracken strode in. "Louise has been teasing me, General," said the president over the shuffling of a dozen people standing up from around the table. "She says you've got good news."

"We've found more of the hostages, sir," said Greffen.

"Oh, thank God," said President Goodson as he settled into his chair and rolled up to the table.

Greffen sat and the other advisors likewise returned to their seats. "We're not one hundred percent certain we've found them all, sir."

Louise McCracken accepted a document from an aid. "How many are we talking?" she said.

"At least fifteen at sites alpha and bravo." Greffen nodded at the map displayed on the big screen. "That leaves as many as five unaccounted for, sir."

The president sighed. "Is there any chance we'll be getting any better intelligence?"

"Mr. President," said McCracken, "it's been three days. We need to move."

President Goodson rubbed his face with his hand. "But I'm the one who'll have to make the call, have to tell some distraught spouse or parent that their loved one isn't coming home."

Greffen leaned forward. "Mr. President, you know I'm personally invested in this, too. I have to go home tonight and look my wife in the eye. She'll be making those same phone calls. Sir, I agree with Louise on this one."

The president nodded slowly and looked up at the map. "How soon can we move, General?"

"Thirty minutes. The teams are already in place."

President Goodson frowned, but finally said, "Alright. Do it."

Greffen looked over his shoulder at the soldier waiting behind him. The aid immediately stepped up to the table, picked up a phone and dialed. After a moment, he wordlessly passed the handset off to Greffen.

Greffen put the handset to his ear. "Operation—" Oh, goddammit. Heads would roll for this. He cleared his throat. "Operation: VANILLA EXTRACT is go."

Chapter 18

FRIDAY

The few strips of yellow police tape fell away as Beretta hauled back the sliding barn door. It glided halfway down its track on inertia alone, allowing a long rectangle of late morning light to reveal the inky splotches that remained from Farmer Jones's last stand.

The barn floor was a dusty mess of boot prints and dried blood, and even at a glance, Beretta could see that a lot of the scuffs and smears were the work of the sheriff and his meager department. They'd shot some photos, taken away the body and closed the door, but tramped all over the place while they were at it. Good thing she didn't need to send Forensics in here.

She took a deep breath, filling her lungs with the myriad aromas of the farm, and just a whiff of iron, and sighed. She crossed the threshold, removing a tiny flashlight from her jacket pocket.

Beretta began to mentally catalog her environment, sweeping the flashlight beam into the shadows, trying and failing to discern Jones's final actions based on the patterns in the dust. But her inspection was on automatic pilot—after all, how much was there to learn here that she didn't know already—while she fixated on a lie she'd told Diane Jones.

Did she know how this had happened? How a fucking monster had turned up on their farm? Who was responsible? Of course she'd said, 'no.' Beretta couldn't do her job without keeping secrets. Lots and lots of secrets. That was easy. Fairly easy. It didn't bother her or eat at her. But that was for national security.

This business with the wasp was different. This was some mega-corporation's little experiment gone awry. Or, worse, maybe their dirty little secret. They'd unleashed a genetic abomination upon an unwitting populace and for what? Darryl Jones's death had been senseless.

Beretta didn't know why Ransom Research Corporation was running this experiment, or what they hoped to accomplish. She didn't have all the answers for Diane Jones— Bullshit! Excuses. She was just trying to talk herself into feeling better about it. That stopped now. She did not throw private pity parties in her head.

General Greffen would seek justice for Darryl, she'd see to that. She'd lean on him, if she had to. But she wouldn't have to lean very hard. And that's why she worked for the man. Why she could carry out his covert missions, keep the ugly secrets, and still sleep soundly at night. Greffen's integrity was unimpeachable.

The ground floor of the barn wasn't sharing any more secrets. Beretta directed the beam of the flashlight up into the hayloft, but from down here there was nothing to see. She unbuttoned her jacket and mounted the ladder.

As she trudged up one rung and the next, the goddamn skirt snatched at her knees. She took to watching the skirt while blindly climbing the ladder, until she finally reached the top.

She looked up and several black and yellow bugs—roughly the size of her hand—looked back at her. "Oh shit!"

Beretta glanced quickly into the hayloft just before it dropped out of sight as she slid down the ladder. The manoeuvre would have been flawlessly executed if she'd been wearing *real* clothes, but her wedge shoes and that fucking skirt conspired together to put her on her ass. Immediately, she pulled a stiletto from a sheath concealed between her shoulder blades, and neatly sliced the first pursuing wasp in half.

She slashed open her skirt, dodged back away from the ladder and onto her feet.

With a droning buzz, several more of the insects bobbed up into the air from the hayloft.

Well this was not at all how Beretta had expected to go out. A swarm of hummingbird-sized manifestations of evil? The hell with that!

She threw a glance over her shoulder at the glowing aperture of the barn door. A goal, for sure, but no guarantee of safety. One step at a time: survive, escape, close the door. And at least she wouldn't be tripping over the damned skirt any more.

She drew an ultra-compact pistol from inside her jacket as she made her break for the door. The wasps emitted a keening whine and zipped after her with worrying speed. Beretta snapped off several rounds, the tiny pistol bucking wildly in her hand.

Chapter 19

FRIDAY

Walter Renford pushed open the door to his condominium, his keys jangling like chimes where they hung from the deadbolt. He shuffled inside, grimacing at the stale, boiled-cabbage smell that made the air feel thick and that was so palpably linked to 'old people' in his mind. This is what he got for hiring that damnable cleaning woman. Bring an old woman into the house, and she drags her old woman smells in with her. Not that Walter could imagine tolerating some kid coming in here, what with their incomprehensible babbling about their interwebs and their car phones full of the Hungry Birds. Bah!

No, he'd get used to the god awful smell in a moment, like he always did. He needed to stay focused, while the idea was still fresh in his mind. He squinted, and his eyes glinted like mid-afternoon light off a polished 'art installation.' An 'art installation' crumpling under the weight of a truck-sized bug. The corners of his mouth twitched up ever so briefly.

He took his hand off his cane, which remained conveniently standing beside him, and slammed the door as he removed his hat. After carefully checking the brim and crown—ever so slightly lopsided from years of service—he hung it on the hat rack by the door. Then he began to shrug his way out of his coat, but paused and sighed. He pulled the coat back on, snatched up his cane, turned and yanked the door open again. His keys jingled mockingly in the lock.

Walter grumbled, fixing them with a steely glare before pulling them from the lock and slamming the door yet again. The bolt made a hollow snap as he threw it home and then returned to the complex dance of shrugging off the coat. Ridiculous really, now that he thought about it, but he hadn't found a decent coat in twenty years. It's like every tailor in the world simultaneously forgot how to make one properly, leaving Walter to struggle out of the accursed things. And if he wasn't careful, he'd be feeling it in his shoulder for the rest of the evening. He blamed the Chinese.

With the coat off and hung beneath his hat, Walter settled back into his usual stooped posture. He shuffled away from the door as he thumbed through his mental rolodex. Blasted Chinese and their garment manufacturing monopolies trying to sidetrack him. He had to get on to this letter-to-the-editor, before some demand or other blunted Walter's edge. After that scene he'd witnessed today, this letter would cut to the quick. Let the editor beware. Yes, sir.

No sooner had he made it out of the foyer and into the living room, the *urge* struck him. He pivoted around his cane, back the way he'd come, naturally, since the nearest bathroom was hardly three feet removed from the front door. At this rate, he'd never make it fully into his damned house. But when nature called, she *called*.

Walter made the return trip to the bathroom in record time, thank God.

The trouble, really, was the coffee. That damnable, lah-di-dah, more-sugar-than-anything-else coffee, and those pretentious, overpriced coffee shops that served it. Not that Walter would ever consider drinking the stuff. Coffee should be percolated. It should hit the tongue like a lump of lead and it should scratch your throat on the way down. Ideally, he would have a *slice* of coffee, rather than a cup of it. No, when Walter got a coffee, it came from a diner. Or the IHOP. But it was still their fault, those damnable coffeehouses.

He flushed and resumed his aborted course, remembering to zip up his fly about halfway through the foyer.

They had corrupted coffee, somehow. Even at the diners. Even the IHOP! Thirty years ago, Walter would take a piss first thing in the morning, and another before bed at night, and he'd drink coffee all the day long in between. But, now? Oh, no. *Now*, it seemed like he was running for the head every five damned minutes. He shook his head.

He finally reached his desk, barren but for a journal, a stack of fresh blank paper, and the steel beast that was his Hermes 3000 manual typewriter.

He stared at it for a moment, waiting for the universe to remind him why he was standing here. "Right," he said. "The letter."

He drew the topmost blank page off the stack—after a moment's resistance to his dry fingertips—and fed it into the machine. The typewriter purred as he rolled the paper into position.

Walter hunted and pecked his way through his name and address. He spent a patient moment carefully peering through his bifocals at his watch, and then added the date. Then, slowly and deliberately, one resounding kerthunk after another, he typed, "Dear Editor-in-Chief, I have recently learned of a matter of no small urgency and dire consequence to our community:"

Walter stopped typing and waited, all the while chewing thoughtfully on his tongue. He stared at the page glassy eyed, trying to conjure to mind the core of the idea that had compelled this particular letter. After a moment, he grunted and nodded, and then he typed, "Fluoride."

Chapter 20

FRIDAY

President Goodson tossed aside a report and sighed. "This waiting is absolutely killing Louise, General."

General Greffen glanced across the table at McCracken, who hadn't bothered to look up from the page she was annotating.

"Oh, she hides it well," said the president. "But she's all raw nerves."

Greffen gave the president a small smile. "The teams should be in place any moment—" A soldier halfway across the room caught his attention with a wave. The man nodded when Greffen made eye contact. "Ah. Looks like it's time, Mr. President." He raised his voice so he'd be heard over the buzz of activity. "Put it on the speaker, son."

Despite Greffen's age, and as much experience as he'd had, it still amazed him just how many butterflies could crowd into his stomach whenever this moment inevitably arrived. And, of course, he had to urinate. It never failed. As soon as he couldn't possibly rush off to the bathroom, that's exactly where his bladder told him to go.

"This is all going to happen very fast, sir," he said to President Goodson.

"I understand, General." The president leaned forward with his elbows on the table. "Not my first rodeo." He laced his fingers together and hid his expression behind his hands.

Greffen wasn't even sure if his bladder was actually full.

A man's voice whispered loudly over the speaker on the conference table, "Alpha team ready."

"Beta team ready," hissed another voice.

Then the field commander barked, "Engage."

The truth, not that he was interested in sharing this with anyone in the room, was that Greffen would really, really like to be somewhere else right now. His body certainly knew it, which was most likely why his bladder was saying, 'hey George, why don't you shuffle on down to the head. It'll only take a minute.'

Sporadic clicks and crackles cut in on the speaker. Greffen knew it was gunfire, though it didn't sound like the hollow booms from the movies, or the crisp pops of real life. But just knowing was enough to raise his heart rate, to start the nervous sweating.

Greffen focused on the documents in front of him. Much as he wanted to close his eyes against the voices on the speaker reporting positions and casualties, that would only pull him deeper into the fantasy of being in the field. He read the words on the pages, holding up the dry, technical language like a shield. Anything to distract him from memories of the heat, and the tightness of the body armor, and the weight of the pistol in his hands. The crunch of splintering wood as he'd kicked in the door. The fear. His fear, as he swept from room to room, searching for combatants. The terror of the occupants, huddled into corners, trying to look small and harmless so he wouldn't hurt them.

"Confirming all clear," said the voice of the field commander.

Greffen took a deep breath, feeling ever so slightly disoriented and very relieved to find a roomful of stern faces looking at him. "It's done, Mr. President," he said and nodded to his aid across the room.

The speaker on the conference table switched off.

"How many hostages were recovered?" said President Goodson.

Greffen's aid, telephone handset pressed tightly to his ear, nodded repeatedly and scribbled notes on a pad. After a long silent moment, he cupped his hand over the phone and said, "Fifteen, sir."

All of the serious faces around the table simultaneously split into wide grins, followed by a din of congratulations and handshaking.

"Well done, General," said the president.

"Thank you, sir." Greffen felt his shoulders ease down a couple of inches. And then his bladder spoke up again. Crap. Not a false alarm after all. Could he make a break for the head, or would the whole Situation Room bear witness to his pee-pee dance?

Chapter 21

FRIDAY

One of the wasps vanished in a spray of goo as Beretta's shots found their mark, but she wasn't pausing to admire her marksmanship. She closed the distance to the barn door in just a few strides, a sinister buzzing somewhere behind but close on her heels.

When she reached the door, she caught the edge with the meat of her palm—stiletto still clenched in her fist—and hooked her body around it and out of the barn. The pursuing insect darted through the door, but came up short, bobbing in the air as it apparently sought it's lost quarry.

They're fast, but dumb and imprecise, thank God. Beretta threw her weight into the door, and set it on course to slam shut. She twisted toward the wasp, instinctively tucking the pistol close to her side, as she would for close-quarters combat. With a pop-pop-pop, the bug became a sticky mist.

Beretta jumped back several long steps, gun held at the ready, eyes dancing over the front of the barn. She held her breath and strained to hear over the hammering of her heart and the rushing of blood in her ears. No whine, no buzz, no vindictive evil hummingbirds in hot pursuit.

She calmed herself with deep breaths and slowly backed down the path away from the barn. The door was closed, and the immediate threat appeared to be over, but the hayloft window gaped open. The building was not secure, she didn't know how many more of them were in there, and time was ticking.

Once Beretta was in front of the house again, she sheathed her stiletto and dropped the magazine from her pistol into her hand. She counted five rounds missing. Shots fired meant paperwork, dammit. She swapped in her other mag and holstered the weapon.

Without taking her eyes off the barn, she extracted her phone from a jacket pocket. She sighed. Her flashlight was still in the barn. That was irritating. "And it was on, too," she mumbled.

She dialed and held the phone to her ear, continuing to grumble while the phone rang. "Battery'll be dead by the time I get it—"

"Greffen," barked the phone.

"Beretta."

"Report."

"Your friend's bug was here, General."

"Well, I'll be damned. You found it?" said Greffen.

Beretta shook her head. "Negative, sir. Just the disaster it left behind. And a bit of a wrinkle, sir."

Greffen didn't reply.

"The bug killed a farmer. Witness says it was nearly as big as a man. And I just encountered three mean little fuckers, sir."

"Are you telling me about mean wasps, soldier?" rumbled Greffen.

Beretta flinched and pulled the phone an extra inch away from her ear. "Yessir. And big," she said. "Maybe as big as a small bird. I caught sight of a nest in the barn before I had to evac."

"Evac?"

"Tactical retreat, sir. There'll be some paperwork."

She heard Greffen sigh into the phone. "You all right, Colonel?"

"Ruined another skirt, sir," she said, looking down at the tattered remains of her uniform for the first time. "When the hell are you going to bring the uniform code into the twenty-first century?"

Greffen chuckled. "Not my jurisdiction. Is the site secure?"

"Negative, General."

"I want an exterminator on the premises yesterday, Colonel. One bug on the loose is enough of a problem."

Beretta swiped at the dust on her uniform with her free hand. "If you don't mind, sir, I'd like to call in my boys. They could be here inside of a few hours."

"Make the call. Seal the barn. Wait for my orders. Do you need anything from me?"

Beretta looked back at the barn and smirked. "I might need you to back date some ordinance requisition forms, General."

"Get it done, Colonel. I'm counting on you." The call ended and the phone beeped in Beretta's ear.

Right now, Woodrow was feeling pretty good. More Adam's apple than brains? Not this time, Roy. Not hardly. He crossed his arms. Then uncrossed them and shoved his hands in his pockets. What with knees and elbows always sticking out every which way, he struggled to find a posture that conveyed how seriously he took this situation. 'Cause it was important, the look of the thing.

But, actually, Woodrow couldn't stop himself grinning like an idiot. He was trying hard not to do it while Roy was looking, though. That was easier with Roy using his binoculars, of course. Roy couldn't catch him smiling while he was peering out at the Jones's farm through those field glasses, no sir.

Not that he shouldn't feel proud of himself. After all, he saw 'er first, and Roy would've been none the wiser.

"Mighty strange to see government types out these parts, eh, Woodrow?" said Roy.

Woodrow nodded to himself. Yessir, seemed like ever since Roy decided they were— they *was* dropping outta high school, Woodrow had been trying to catch up. And finally—

"Eh?" said Roy.

Woodrow started. "Don't seem right, Roy. And a woman, at that," he said.

Roy lowered the binoculars a few inches and glanced over his shoulder at his friend. "Now Woodrow, there ain't *nothin'* wrong with a woman in uniform."

Woodrow's face felt hot and his stomach filled up with butterflies. Now he'd done it. Said the wrong damn thing. Again. Like an idiot. But he could still fix it, turn it back around, say something smart. "I bet— I bet they have their uses?"

Roy continued to watch Woodrow, one eyebrow slowly rising.

"Somebody's gotta mend torn clothes and fix meals out on the battlefield, eh, Roy?"

Roy lowered his arms and turned to face Woodrow.

Oh shit oh shit oh shit.

"Woodrow, that's the most insensitiving thing ya coulda said. What would them government types think if they heard ya?"

Ohshit ohshit ohshit!

Just before total panic could sweep away Woodrow's frozen smile, Roy barked out a vicious laugh. He rested the binoculars against the belly he'd been growing for all the years Woodrow had known him.

Woodrow chuckled, too. Reflexes like a cat, yessiree.

Roy turned back to the Jones's farm and held up the binoculars again. "Get the boys together," he said. "They'll wanta know 'bout this business."

Chapter 22

FRIDAY

Five years. Five years on the project, and without so much as a 'Nice job, Stuart,' and a pat on the back, he'd been reassigned. Doctor Stuart Rhys-Billingsly glanced over from his computer screen to the empty table top where the specimens had been. One little miscalculation. It was only off by, like, ten thousand, no more than one hundred thousand times. An easy enough thing to fix in the next iteration. If he could still get to his notes, which he apparently couldn't. Nope. Just a 'take a sick day,' and back to an empty lab.

Not that they'd still be sitting there now, anyway. By now each one would be too big to fit through the door. He could only hope that Doctor Zmeyansky had the good sense to destroy— Nope, best not to think about that. None of his concern anymore. He'd done what he could about that and it was officially no longer his problem. And he would not be thinking about that anymore, not one bit—and holy gods one of them might be out there somewhere—no, one plus one makes two plus one makes three plus two makes five plus three makes eight plus five makes thirteen. By the time Stuart reached nine hundred eighty-seven he was able to carefully steer his attention back to his computer.

Hymenopteran mouthparts. More robust hymenopteran mouthparts, to be more precise. Why they'd want him researching *that* was anyone's guess. Millions of years of evolution made the mandibles of the parasitic wasp species powerful enough to easily dismember the armored bodies of their prey. Wasn't that robust enough? But Stuart wasn't in the habit of worrying about why. His interest was much more focused on 'could it be done.' He let other people figure out what to do with the results.

He tapped the spacebar to advance another page and then returned to absentmindedly scratching his injured hand. It was raw and puffy, but much improved. He didn't even wince as he plunged it into his pocket to dig out his buzzing phone.

Gods, what a troll. Or perhaps the guy posting in this thread was just an idiot. Ranting about using a Minkelson ZA15 pressure micrometer to measure chewing strength. How big did he think a paper wasp was? Clearly, the Belstrom KR67 was the proper tool. He shook his head, looked down at the glowing screen of his phone, and felt like someone had kicked him in the gut.

Stuart's finger trembled as he answered the call. "George, how nice to hear from you?"

General Greffen's voice burbled in his ear. "Was that a question, Stuart?"

"Any chance you're calling about cookies?"

"'fraid not."

Stuart sighed.

"Listen, Stuart, I could use some advice. We found your bug."

"Oh, good?"

"You're sounding a little uncertain, Stuart."

Stuart slumped forward and held his head in his free hand. "Honestly, George, I'm feeling a little conflicted."

"Well, you should have some time to ponder that in the car."

"Car?"

"Yup. There's one waiting for you in the parking lot. I'll see you soon."

Stuart cast about desperately for a response, his tongue waggling silently.

The phone beeped. George had hung up.

—nine hundred eighty-seven plus six hundred ten makes one thousand five hundred ninety-seven plus nine hundred eighty-seven makes—

Stuart closed his laptop and retrieved his bag.

Chapter 23

FRIDAY

"She's almost ready to start walking. Furniture surfing, climbing up your pant leg at every opportunity. Here, I've got the cutest picture." Fudley flicked through photos on his phone.

Luile sat in the driver's seat beside Fudley, hands firmly gripping the wheel at ten and two, eyes front and jaw set. With his blond buzz cut, three days worth of stubble, and a mountain of muscle thinly covered by a dark gray mock-turtle, he could've just stepped off an action movie set. "Put the phone away, Fud."

Fudley continued to poke at his phone. "Just a sec, I've almost found it." He teased his handlebar mustache with his free hand.

"Knock it off, Fud."

Fudley looked over at Luile. "What's your problem?"

Luile spared Fudley the briefest of sidelong glances before turning back to the road. "We're on our way to an op. Are you looking to get yourself killed?"

"What the hell are you—?"

From the back seat, Yonda joined the conversation. "He's right, Fud. Better put it away."

Fudley leaned around his seat so he could see Yonda. "Et tu, Brutae?"

Yonda shook his head and crossed his arms over his own gray turtleneck, similarly bursting with pectorals. "It's a jinx, Fud. You don't show family pics to your buddies right before an op. Even New Guy, here, knows it." He thrust his chin out at the giant occupying the rest of the back of the SUV.

"Really?" said Bhalsim. "'New Guy?' What am I, some green recruit fresh from training?"

Yonda chuckled. "Sorry, man," he said. "We don't exactly get a lot of new blood around here."

Bhalsim nodded thoughtfully, and said, "They're right, Fudley. It's a jinx."

Fudley sighed and slipped his phone back into his trouser pocket. "Fine. But you're missing out. Cutest. Kid. In. The. World." He looked out the windshield for a moment, then studied the scenery as it zipped past, then examined the dashboard of the Escalade, all the while his fingers dancing on his thighs in ever greater agitation. "So," he said finally, "how do you know Cody, Bhalsim? And what the hell kind of soldier gets laid up playing golf? Anybody? Anybody?"

Luile growled, "Clearly you've never seen the man golf."

Bhalsim nodded his agreement. "I've known Cody since all the way back in basic. We did a tour together in Afghanistan. Crossed paths a few times since. Stayed in touch. Still, bit of a surprise when I got the call about this."

"Well," said Fudley. "I guess if Cody vouched for you, and Greffen's Scalpel picked you, you can't be all bad." He held out his fist. "Welcome to the team."

Bhalsim rapped knuckles with Fudley. "Greffen's Scalpel?"

"Beretta. The CO."

Yonda shook his head and laughed. "Man, you know you're the only one who calls her that, right?"

"It'll catch on sooner or later, you'll see," said Fudley.

Yonda rolled his eyes.

"What?" continued Fudley. "It's clever."

Bhalsim shook his head. "Ok, I don't get it."

Fudley laughed. "Did Cody tell you anything about what you were getting into?"

"No. They kind of frown on you talking about this kind of work."

"Ha ha!" Fudley clapped his hands. "He really threw you to the wolves, didn't he?"

Bhalsim did not look amused.

"Ok, ok," continued Fudley. "So you know that back—oh, I don't know—around the time the wheel was invented, maybe, General Greffen was a medic, right? Right."

"The man's not that old," grumbled Luile.

"Says the old geezer," said Fudley, his mustache jiggling mischievously.

"I'm only two years older than you."

"*Anyway*, our CO, Beretta, she solves the tough problems for him with surgical precision. So, you know, Greffen's Scalpel."

Bhalsim nodded quietly for a long moment. "Right," he said. "Yeah, not so sure that's gonna stick."

Fudley shrugged. "Well, even so, it annoys the hell out of her when I say it, so it's all good."

Yonda chuckled, and then the group settled into silence for a minute.

Finally, Bhalsim said, "So, Beretta. What's she like? I've never had a woman for a CO before."

With a sound like gravel in a coffee can, Luile laughed. "Oh, you'll see," he growled.

Chapter 24

FRIDAY

Senior Airman Boguslaw "Bogey" Aaltink fidgeted on a bench at the mall. Bright sunshine filtered down from skylights overhead onto planter boxes full of vibrant green plants—possibly even real—creating a park-like atmosphere. Behind him, a fountain burbled, a relaxing oasis for the weary shopper. It wasn't working on Bogey. Not today.

He'd followed their instructions to the letter. Wandering around that ridiculous bookstore like he was really shopping. Who the hell bought paper books anymore? Clearly, nobody around here did. He'd been the only customer in the store the whole time. He should've picked out something ironic, like 'I Made a Million Dollars Without Really Trying, and So Can You!' That would have been worth a chuckle, later on when he could relax a bit. But with his nerves wound this tight, it was all he could do to grab a random dummy-do-it-yourself-help-whatever book without totally looking like he was up to something. Well, it was big and heavy, which was what they wanted. But twenty dollars! Just remember, the money doesn't matter. There'll be plenty of money, soon enough. He'd had the clerk put it in a bag, just like they'd told him. And then he'd plunked down on this bench to wait. And fidget.

"Sir!" said a voice, startling him.

Bogey looked up to see the stern face of a mall cop—no, a real cop, just here in the mall—looking down on him from his stupid electric scooter. Bile quickly rose in Bogey's throat, but he swallowed it down, and followed the cops pointing finger. The no smoking sign. He looked down at his hands and realized he was seconds away from lighting up. He shook his head. His hands must have gone on auto-pilot.

"Sorry, officer," he said, adding a nervous laugh. He tucked the unlit cigarette back into the packet with trembling fingers. The cop moved on and Bogey took a deep, shaky breath.

He looked down at the bag from the bookstore, and then at the bag containing his sandwich that lay beside it. He couldn't eat it. He'd throw up. And that would be 'deviating' from the instructions.

He'd managed to take all of about three bites like an hour ago, right after he'd bought it. And then nerves got the better of him, and he'd wrapped it back up again.

Sandwich Artist. That's the title they gave to the old woman behind the counter who'd slapped the thing together for him. This is what was wrong with America today! Had that old woman been working dead end jobs like that her whole life? Or was she forced back out there, so late in life, to make freaking sandwiches to pay the bills? And then they call her a Sandwich Artist. It's dressing up the pig, right? No one with that title is an artist, they're just underpaid, unskilled labor, going nowhere. The American Dream is dead, only no one notices because the marketing is too damned good.

Just look at his folks. They came to America, saddled him with this old-country name, and worked their fingers to the bone to achieve the Dream. And they're so thankful for all the wonderful opportunities, even though they're still working, well into their seventies. They can't see it.

And what kind of American Dream did he ever get, huh? Career military only without the career part. He put in the work, out in the sun, just like they told him to. Only then the doc tells him that freckle between his eyes isn't a freckle after all. Ten seconds with a scalpel later, and he's a goddamned cancer survivor. Which turned out to mean he stayed an Airman for thirty years, doing pretty much the same damned thing, grinding through the same motions. Wash, rinse, repeat. That was it. No climbing the ranks. No career path. No perks. Not even a skill he could take to some civilian profession. Well, not a profession he'd want, anyway. And at his age who wanted to start over?

The American Dream was dead, if it ever existed to begin with. A guy had to take what he wanted, whenever he could. Just look at all the cutthroat corporations. Screw everybody, Bogey Aaltink was finally gonna get his—

Another bookstore bag appeared alongside Bogey's. He looked over as a man in an expensive-looking black suit and round rimmed glasses settled onto the bench. Round-rims didn't spare Bogey a glance.

Nausea washed over him again, but it was now or never. Moment of truth. Time to grab life by the balls. Or something. Whatever. Bogey stood up, snatching up Round-rims's bag as he did so. His face felt flush, and it was everything he could do not to run or look over his shoulder every three feet. He was halfway back to the parking garage when he realized he'd left his sandwich on the bench.

Nevermind. He could afford a lot of sandwiches now. Wonder if Mr. Round-rims likes bologna and American cheese.

Chapter 25

FRIDAY

By the time her boys finally showed up at the Jones's farm in their shiny black SUV, Beretta had traded what was left of that restrictive joke of a dress uniform for her *real* service gear. Whatever the brass might say about dress code, Beretta wasn't convinced it was real military attire if she didn't feel comfortable wearing it to infiltrate hostile territory and neutralize enemy warlords. But now that the soft-touch meeting with the grieving widow was over, she could slip into her dark gray Dickies and mock-turtle. These clothes hugged her body like a second skin, wouldn't restrict her movement or reveal her position. The fact that she looked damn fine in them was merely an added bonus.

Beretta finished strapping a pair of M9s to her thighs while the boys extricated themselves and a handful of gear from their ride. She kept her eye on

Bhalsim, who practically unfolded as he exited the vehicle. Bringing on a new team member was exciting, and annoying, and a little bit dangerous, given their line of work. Curse Cody for selfishly going on medical leave. And she was only half kidding about that, even if she was being a terrible person for thinking it.

She'd vetted Bhalsim, of course. He had Cody's recommendation, which was pretty huge, and a resume that backed it up. So she was getting a first-class professional. But would he be a temp or a lifer? A lot of that would be down to personality—whether his clicked with theirs. Would he laugh at her jokes? Would he be like Fudley—no. No, the world was not a big enough place to house two Fudleys.

In short order, her team was standing at attention on the dusty gravel drive.

Beretta crossed her arms. "Well, boys," she said, "I've got a doozy for you today. This is so far out there that even Fudley here wouldn't have dreamt it up."

"Tell me it's crop circles, ma'am. I've got twenty bucks riding on it," said Fudley.

"You lost your twenty, Fud. At dawn on Wednesday, Farmer Jones was torn limb from limb in that barn back there—" she gestured with her thumb over her shoulder "—by a goddamn killer mutant wasp nearly as big as he was." Beretta noticed the surprise that flickered across Bhalsim's face, before he squelched it. The rest of her team didn't bat an eye.

"I should've brought the RPGs," growled Luile. He squinted at the rust-colored barn menacingly.

"But you brought the other ordinance I requested?" said Beretta.

Luile nodded. "Yes, ma'am."

"Good. The bug is no longer here; current whereabouts unknown. But it left behind a present: a nest."

Fudley grinned broadly.

Beretta rested her hands idly on the grips of her pistols and continued, "Our mission is to contain that barn, prevent any mutant wasps from escaping and ravaging the countryside, and await further orders. Or, as Fudley would say, 'just another typical Friday.' I want full body armor, tactical shotguns with frangibles. If you need to put down a wasp, I don't want you making a new exit. Understood?"

The men called out a chorus of 'Yes, ma'am's and one 'yessir.'

Beretta rounded on Bhalsim, like a shark smelling blood. Today just might be a fun day after all. "Did you just 'yessir' me, soldier?"

Bhalsim didn't look at Beretta, instead keeping his eyes leveled on the horizon, and a good two feet over her head. "Yess—er," he said.

"Cody led me to believe that you were a sharp one, soldier. I thought that included knowing the difference between a man and a woman. Was there something about these tits—" Beretta pointed at her chest "—that confused you, soldier?"

Bhalsim's gaze shifted from the horizon to Beretta and back in a millisecond. "N-no, s—ma'am," he said.

"Oh, so you did notice these curves, did you soldier?"

"Y—yes, ma'am?"

Beretta stepped in close, the disparity in their heights suddenly much less noticeable. "Have you been staring at my ass soldier?!"

At the very moment that a look of total panic appeared on Bhalsim's face, Fudley completely busted a gut.

Shit. "Fudley!" shouted Beretta.

Fudley hunched over, gradually easing down from a guffaw to some giggles. At last he managed to say, "Sorry, ma'am. I just couldn't hold it in any longer."

Beretta shook her head. "Dammit, Fud. You ruined it. I had him right where I wanted him."

"My bad, ma'am."

Bhalsim still had a hunted look on his face. "Ma'am?" he said.

Beretta eased off a step, fixing Bhalsim with an appraising stare. "All kidding aside, Bhalsim, it's ma'am or Colonel. I've got no need to pretend I'm just one of the boys. Clear?"

"Crystal, ma'am!"

Beretta smiled. The answer to that question had been drilled into these men since basic training. She could always count on it to shift them back into drive. "Alright," she said, "move it!"

Half crouched, Woodrow crept up behind Roy, who was hunkered down beside the disc of Woodrow's massive John Deere. He couldn't help but wonder why he should have to sneak around on *his* farm, amongst *his* equipment, but he damn well wasn't gonna embarrass himself by asking Roy about that. He took the last half-dozen steps on exaggerated tippy toes, which somehow seemed right, considering all the crouching.

"There's more of 'em, now," said Roy, hunched awkwardly behind the disc, and watching the movements of the soldiers on the Jones's farm through Woodrow's binoculars.

"What they doin', Roy?" said Woodrow.

Roy glanced back at Woodrow, who was half-standing behind him, neck craned forward and hand up to shield his eyes from the late day sun. Roy grabbed a fistful of Woodrow's shirt and yanked. "Would you get down, you idjit?"

Woodrow stumbled down into a squat, narrowly catching himself on the frame of the disc, instead of one of its sharper protrusions. "Sorry— sorry, Roy." He waited a moment as Roy studied the action with the binoculars. "Well, Roy, what they doin'?"

"Dunno," said Roy. "Something to the barn." He scratched at the stubble on his chin. "I don't like it."

Woodrow's calves were starting to twinge from the awkward position. "I got the boys together back at my house," said Woodrow in a stage whisper. The stage whisper felt more appropriate, what with the sneaking, and it was important to Woodrow that he get this right, even if he was too dim to understand the necessity of it.

"Alright. Let's go have a chat," said Roy. He shuffled backward without looking away from the Jones's farm. He promptly bumped into Woodrow, who tumbled to his butt with a crunch of the gravel. Roy looked at Woodrow and sighed. "Idjit."

Roy and Woodrow came through the door, and the low murmur of conversation ceased.

Woodrow's little dining room felt unusually tight and stuffy, filled with the eight other men that collectively referred to themselves as the Mayhew County Militia. Most sat around the dining table, a few resting their heads on their calloused hands, and a couple of rifles were leaned against the table between the chairs. To a man, they wore their typical uniform of boots, denim, flannel and dust.

Dwayne, solid as a rock and easily the most intimidating member of the militia, pushed himself out of the corner where he'd been leaning. He loomed.

Woodrow was pretty sure that was the word for it. Dwayne was a loomer, he was. Always looming at people. Woodrow instinctively leaned back a smidge, even though, strictly speaking, being all the way across the room put him out of looming range. Which must be a thing, right? Someone must have figured out just how far one could loom—

Dwayne said, "What's goin' on out there, Roy?"

"Somethin's up with the Jones's?" said old Jimmy from his seat at the table.

Owen lifted his head off his hands and leaned back in his chair beside Jimmy. "Damn shame about ol' Darryl," he said.

Roy's baby-faced brother Zach piped up, "The Sheriff, he said—"

"There's government types up at the Jones's," said Roy.

Woodrow saw his chance to contribute and leapt for it. "There's a woman!" he said.

"You call us out here just 'cause of a woman?" said Jimmy. He scowled at Woodrow.

Woodrow colored, thinking furiously for a reply.

"She ain't alone," said Roy.

Woodrow breathed a sigh of relief as Jimmy shifted his attention to Roy.

Roy continued, "Brought some soldiers out there, too."

"They're messing—" Woodrow swallowed, his Adam's apple bobbing urgently. "*They's* messin' with the Jones's barn," he said. Woodrow held his breath in anticipation of another rebuke. But surely *barns* weren't controversial; not like *women*.

Owen sighed. "Damn shame about ol' Darryl," he said.

Zach tried again. "The Sheriff, he said—"

"What the hell's the government want with the Jones's barn?" said Dwayne. He folded his arms and loomed out of his corner of the room a bit more.

Woodrow felt himself involuntarily lean away from Dwayne. Maybe he'd made a misapprehension about maximum looming ranges. "It doesn't make any—

" He cleared his throat. "It don't make no sense, it don't, eh, Dwayne?" Woodrow laughed nervously.

"Well the Sheriff, he said—"

"Damn shame about ol' Darryl," said Owen, shaking his head.

"Ol' Darryl," said Jimmy, staring unseeingly across the table, "he was complainin' just the other day—"

Dwayne nodded. "That's right—"

Jimmy continued, "—said his seed man was after him 'bout next year's crop—"

Dwayne moved his hands to his belt loops. "No, he was sayin' his tax refund—"

"—wants him to order them new-fangled seeds," said Jimmy.

Dwayne balled his hands into fists, knuckles white. "—government still had his money and they weren't payin'."

Woodrow knew what to say about that. "Government!" He shook his head disparagingly.

"Them altered seeds, ya know," said Jimmy, bringing his eyes back into focus and looking from face to face.

Roy grunted. "Well, that's ol' Darryl for ya."

"Damn shame about ol' Darryl." Owen rubbed his chin.

Zach's ruddy face ping-ponged from speaker to speaker, until, for an instant, there was no reply. He half-heartedly said, "Well, the Sheriff, he said—"

"What's that, Zach?" said Roy.

All eyes turned to Zach, and for a moment he was dumbstruck. "Well, the Sheriff, see," Zach said slowly, the spinning of the gears in his head plain as day on his face. "He, uh, he said it was damn strange, how ol' Darryl died." Zach hesitated, his lips silently replaying his last statement as he apparently studied the ceiling. Finally, he nodded and grinned.

Jimmy shrugged. "I heard Diane shot up the place," he said.

"Don't send no government types just 'cause Diane shot up the place," said Dwayne.

Woodrow found himself nodding furiously, as if hoping his agreement would appease the rage he saw smoldering behind Dwayne's eyes.

"Sheriff didn't say ol' Darryl got shot. No, sir," said Zach, looking smug.

Owen rested his elbows on the table and steepled his fingers. "Damn shame about ol' Darryl," he said.

Woodrow's face lit up as a light bulb popped on in his mind. "Could be government killed Darryl," he said. Suddenly, it was all starting to make sense.

"Can't trust the government to leave you in peace no more," said Dwayne, squeezing his right fist in his left hand, his knuckles cracking like a shot.

The other militiamen nodded and traded knowing looks with each other as they muttered.

"Rhubarb," muttered Woodrow, nodding like the others.

Jimmy spoke up. "Could be government doesn't want us to know what killed ol' Darryl."

"Maybe they's testin' somethin' out there at the Jones's," said Woodrow. The government's treachery increasingly became an open book to him.

Roy held up his hands to quiet the room, his expression calm and sober. "Truth is fellahs, we don't know why they's out at the Jones's." He shrugged casually. "Maybe they gettin' ready to come at us, just usin' the Jones's as a base."

Woodrow hadn't even considered that! And in light of the wide-eyed glances and the significantly louder grumbling amongst his comrades, maybe no one else had worked that out yet, either. His throat felt kinda dry as he raised his voice a little and said, "Rhubarb rhubarb."

Roy continued in his casual, offhand way. "Maybe Jimmy's right and they out there to cover up what happened to ol' Darryl. Some government experiment gone awry."

The others began to shift restlessly, their voices getting ever louder. How could Roy stay so relaxed as he dropped these heinous revelations on them? Woodrow said, "Rhubarb rhubarb."

Roy glanced at Woodrow, a flicker of annoyance on his face, before he continued, "Or maybe that experiment, it went just as they 'spected it would."

The men raised their voices as they spoke over each other.

Woodrow raised his voice, too. "Rhubarb rhubarb!" he said.

Roy, smiling to himself as his compatriots got fired up, snapped his attention to Woodrow, the smile swallowed by a wave of irritation. "Dammit, Woodrow, are you sayin' 'rhubarb rhubarb?'"

"Er, yeah, Roy."

"Why the hell would you be sayin' 'rhubarb' at a time like this?"

Woodrow blushed as all the agitated eyes in the room settled on him. "Well, Roy, you remember as I was in that play with the community theater last season," he said. He looked down at the floor and scratched at the back of his head. "And, well, the director, he told us that when we did the big angry crowd scene, we should say 'rhubarb rhubarb.' 'Cause, you know, it sounds right with the big crowd, and all." He looked back up at Roy. "And since we were— we was all muttering, and— Sorry, Roy."

Roy sighed and shook his head. He looked up at the ceiling, like he was trying to think where he'd left off in his speech. "Probably no use in speculatin' about the why of the thing," he said, finally. "But they's mighty interested in that barn, there—"

"That's right. They's all over that barn," said Woodrow.

Roy fixed Woodrow with an icy stare. "I say, since they want that barn, we should take it first." He glanced around the room at the other men. "We can't have no government types comin' in here and stompin' on our rights. We gotta stand up." He shook a fist in the air. "Keep the government out of our business, I say. We'll show 'em who the real men are that make this country great."

The men shouted their assent, some even thumping Woodrow's table.

"Let's do it for ol' Darryl, fellahs," said Roy. "Let's take that barn!"

The volume in the room rose to a dull roar as the men all shouted at each other and over each other. Zach knocked his chair over as he stood. Dwayne gesticulated menacingly. Owen shook his head, mouthing something indistinctly about "ol' Darryl."

Roy nodded and smiled broadly.

Woodrow, relieved to no longer be the center of attention, shook his head. It just seemed like such a shame, really, that Roy wouldn't let him do this right. To hell with it. How often would he get to play a role in an angry crowd scene, anyway. "Rhubarb, rhubarb, rhubarb," he said quietly.

Chapter 26

SATURDAY

Bogey Aaltink sat in the cab of his truck, staring at the green metal thermos on the seat beside him, trying to understand just what the hell he was doing. He was getting a leg up, is what he was doing. He was doing the easiest thing in the world, and finally he was getting paid. Really paid. Hell, he was gonna be rich. But it just didn't make any kind of sense.

Yesterday at the mall, he'd practically run back to his car after the hand-off. He must have checked the mirrors about forty-five times before he'd worked up the courage to peek in the bag. The thermos and a cell phone.

They'd told him not to open the package. To wait for more instructions after the hand-off. It was like ignoring an itch. The more he didn't scratch it, the more he thought about it. But in the end, he hadn't opened the damn thing. Not with how much they were paying him.

Shit, for that kind of money, with all this hush-hush spy movie crap, there could be something really dangerous in there. He sure as hell wasn't going to let curiosity kill this cat, not with a payday within his grasp. At least, that's how he'd settled things in his mind last night.

They'd called him this morning. Told him what to do with the fucking thing. He'd been turning it over in his head ever since, and any which way he came at it, he just couldn't see the logic of it. But Bogey wasn't getting paid to understand. He was getting paid to walk it past security—which he did, and the MPs hadn't given it a second glance—and then to—

The truck radio gurgled at him, snapping him from his reverie. Bogey grabbed the mic clipped to the side of the ceiling mounted unit. "Birdseed here," he said.

"Birdseed, proceed to area six," said the bored tones of a man's voice on the radio. "Refuel Air Force One."

"Area six. Understood." Bogey hung up the mic and started up the truck, which vroomed to life. The diesel engine caused everything in the cab to vibrate.

And there it was. The call they told him would come. All he had to do was add the contents of the thermos to the fuel and do his job. But it didn't make any sense.

Bogey put the truck in gear and headed off down the tarmac. He couldn't help stealing glances at the thermos sitting there accusingly. But there was just no way that it could damage the plane. Anything he added to that much fuel would be so diluted that it couldn't possibly make any difference, right? Not that he wanted to know. He couldn't feel guilty if he didn't actually know anything. No, he'd just do his part. Get his pay day. If it worked or if it didn't, that wasn't Bogey's problem.

He was definitely getting his money. Enough being the lowly, unappreciated, where-the-hell-have-you-been fuel guy. Hell, they didn't even fly him anywhere. He just watched the planes come and go while he stayed on the ground. Enough. Bogey Aaltink was finally getting his.

He pulled the truck up alongside Air Force One and squeezed the wheel in his sweaty palms. Well, do or die time. He grinned, his face a mask of fear, because he let that last thought slip, the one idea he'd been clamping down on, actively trying not to consider. What if it was all a trick? What if something terrible happened the moment he opened the thermos.

He picked up the bullet-shaped canister, feeling the cold metal under his fingers. It wouldn't make any sense. Nobody important would be near the plane right now. There just wouldn't be any point to—Bogey's mouth felt so dry—blowing it up. And this little thing couldn't be a bomb. It was so small, so light, went slosh like there was liquid inside. Even if it were a bomb, they couldn't be sure it would work. They couldn't know that it would actually damage the plane. It was too unpredictable.

No, Bogey was going to be just fine. He climbed out of the truck, thermos in hand, and made his way around to the fuel line. No, the only thing he needed to worry about from here on out was how to spend all that money.

Jessica leaned back in the supple leather of the recliner aboard Air Force One, watching out the window as another jet rocketed down the nearby runway. A steady stream of her sorority sisters filed down the aisle, giggling and squealing like middle schoolers. She pressed her phone tighter against her ear to block out the din. "What was that, Daddy?" she said.

The President's voice clanged like he was talking into a tin can. "I said, I'm sorry, sweetheart, but Louise says I can't go. Some nonsense about running the country."

Jessica chuckled. "Gee, Daddy, that's really too bad," she said in a tone that indicated that it really wasn't. "It won't be the same without you."

"I have no doubt," he said.

They both laughed.

"Have a fun trip."

"I will," said Jessica.

"Stay out of trouble."

"I will."

"Don't talk to any boys."

"Daddy!"

President Goodson laughed. "Alright, alright. I love you."

"Love you, too," said Jessica. She hung up and looked around the cabin. Most of the girls had been shunted on down the aisle because of the limited seating up here. Courtney was already nose deep in a book. Mandy, Celeste, Britney and Harmony had their eyes glued to their phones, texting each other by the look of it.

The PA system cut on and a man's voice, with a cadence and tone so stereotypical that they must teach it in flight school, said, "This is your captain, Colonel Jonathan Pritchard of the United States Air Force, speaking. On behalf of myself and the flight crew, I'd like to welcome Miss Goodson and the ladies of Kappa Lambda Omega sorority to Air Force One. We've been given clearance to take off and should be in the air in ten minutes. Please stow your luggage and fasten your seatbelts. We'll be landing at Edwards Air Force Base near sunny Los Angeles, California in approximately six hours, where it's a balmy eighty-five degrees."

Chapter 27

SATURDAY

With a final burst of effort, she slowed her descent—her massive wings whipping up a cloud of dust—and crashed down into the field of saplings, crushing many of them with wet snapping noises. The stiff branches scraped harmlessly, but annoyingly, at her armored belly. She turned herself toward the nearby building that had attracted her attention from the air, her lumbering body uprooting a number of the trees as she did so. Wasp-self peered at the structure with her grainy, mosaic-vision and seethed. Looking at things made her so angry.

The building had smelled so attractive from the air, but now that she'd landed, it seemed disappointingly small. *Buzz, thorax-waggle—*

Her thoughts were rudely interrupted by the squealing sound of a non-wasp creature somewhere nearby. "I can't see it. Can you see it?"

"Slow down or I'm telling Mom," vocalized another non-wasp creature. "I don't see nothin'. You didn't see no helicopter."

"I *didn't* see no helicopter. I *heard* it."

"Well, I don't see nothin'. You're just makin' stuff up."

"I'm not makin' stuff up. I heard it. It was super loud and stuff."

Fuming, Wasp-self moved quietly along the side of the building, searching for the non-wasp creatures. *Zig-zagging flight two body lengths long!!* That would teach those non-wasp creatures. She reached the edge of the building and peeked around the corner, spotting a pair of tiny non-wasp creatures in the clearing beyond. The existence of non-wasp creatures pissed her off.

"Well it's got to be here somewhere—oh, dude, check that out." The small non-wasp creature extended one of its limbs.

"What?" vocalized the other non-wasp creature.

"Up in the tree. Bet you a dollar I can hit it." The non-wasp creature touched its limb to the ground, and then something flew away from the creature and into a nearby tree.

To fly backward for three body lengths!!! A burst of scent and color revealed a nest of wasp-others in the tree. The flying object clattered off a branch beside the nest and several agitated wasp-others came out to investigate.

A *thorax-waggle* nest of wasp-others?! This close to the *high-pitched-buzzing* potential new home she came down here to build?!

Another missile clattered off the tree branches.

Dip of the head and a zig-zagging flight of five *body lengths!!!!* This would not stand any longer! Wasp-self lifted her huge body into the air with a deafening whop-whop-whop of her wings.

Suddenly, Wasp-self's senses sparkled with the most intoxicating aroma. She looked toward the sky, tracking a pinprick of vibrant purple as it streaked across the heavens. Nothing had ever seemed so attractive, so mesmerizing. *The touching of the thorax to the ground four times rapidly.*

She absolutely had to catch that fleeting, wonderful object *and destroy it!!!!!*

Wasp-self burned with hatred for the sleek, silver non-wasp creature flying ahead of her. The violet cloudburst of euphoric, rage-inducing perfume that it sprayed behind it compelled her to follow. Her wings ached with the effort of flying so fast for so long, and that made her very grumpy. Catching a non-wasp creature in flight was a *mandible-gnashing* pain in the *thorax-waggle* ovipositor.

With one final burst of speed, Wasp-self closed the distance to the creature. She twisted in the air, hooked her legs around it's stiff, outstretched limbs, and, with pile-driving force, thrust her stinger into the creature's underside.

The rubbing of her hind legs together that was satisfying. This non-wasp creature had teased and tantalized her for too long, and for that it would pay dearly. For that, her wasp-offspring would feast on it's guts while it lived and suffered!

"—and then, from about two stalls over, I hear this epic slosh."

Colonel Pritchard held his cup of coffee an inch from his lips, the impending sip momentarily forgotten while his copilot, Lieutenant Colonel Rogelio Tucker, spun out his yarn.

"And I don't just mean that satisfying splash from a hard-won turd," continued Tucker. "I'm telling you I heard water hitting the tile floor. Whatever happened in there, we're talking lasting consequences, right? And then this man's voice—the most gentle and patient, fatherly voice—intones—and, I mean, *intones*, what with all the echo off the tile and everything—anyway, he says, 'You give *to* the toilet. You do not *get from* the toilet.'"

Pritchard chuckled.

"I know, right?" said Tucker, laughing. "Of course, I'm thinking, there's got to be a father and his little kid in there. But still, pretty amusing."

Pritchard brought the coffee cup to his lips, but hesitated as Tucker held up a finger.

"Not thirty seconds later, the toilet flushes, the door opens, and there's just a guy in a three-piece suit. Not another soul—"

The plane shuddered like they'd just hit a speed bump while doing sixty. Pritchard's coffee spilled over his hand and down his crisp white shirt. "Shit," he said.

Tucker turned his attention back to the instrumentation. "That was strange," he said.

Pritchard set the half-empty cup aside, flicking a few drops of coffee off his hand and onto the floor behind him. He flipped a switch on the console in front of him and spoke into his headset while he dabbed at his shirt with a handy napkin. "Sorry about the bump, there, ladies. We're experiencing some slight turbulence, so if you could return to your seats and fasten your seatbelts for the next few minutes, we'd appreciate it." He turned off the PA, and sighed as he mopped at the coffee.

"We've got a warning light on the nose gear hydraulics, sir," said Tucker.

Pritchard frowned and looked at the display screen where a red icon had lit up. He rapped on the glass with a knuckle, as though the indicator on the screen might've gotten stuck, and sighed. "Dammit," he said. "What do you think, Roge?"

Tucker shook his head. "It's probably nothing. And we are halfway to Edwards already."

Pritchard stared at the screen thoughtfully for a moment, and said, "Yeah, we'll sort it out at Edwards. Wouldn't want to disappoint our passengers, would we?" He adjusted the position of his headset mic and flipped a switch on the console. "Control, this is Air Force One.

Be advised, we have a nose gear hydraulic warning indicator. Over."

A crackly voice came back over the radio with a practiced and professional lack of urgency. "Roger, Air Force One. Will you be making an emergency landing? Over."

"Negative, Control. We'll sort it out when we reach Edwards Air Force Base. Over."

"Roger that, Air Force One," said the voice on the radio. "Fly safe. Control out."

Chapter 28

SATURDAY

President Goodson darted down the White House corridors, his long legs and powerful stride blurring the line between walking and running. Beside him, but only just barely, Louise McCracken half-jogged, half-skipped. She was not so blessed in stature and certainly not dressed for athletic endeavors, and the president could hear her wheezing.

"Mr. President," she hissed.

The voice of the experienced politician screamed in his head. He shouldn't be moving so fast. Just imagine what the next news cycle would look like if any reporters saw him running through the halls. And he should have some mercy on poor Louise.

But fatherhood trumped politics when his baby girl was in trouble. The fact that he wasn't *actually* running would have to be good enough. He burst through the door to the Situation Room, startling some of the men and women inside, and putting a frown on General Greffen's face.

Louise barreled in behind him and narrowly avoided a collision as the president stopped short. "Mr. President—"

"General," said President Goodson. "There's something wrong with my airplane?"

General Greffen stood up from the table, glancing down at the president's balled fists. He sighed. "It's just a warning light, Mr. President."

"Warning lights are there to *warn* you, General. I don't *want* warnings, General." President Goodson's hands began to rise. "I *want* my airplane to behave like a *proper* airplane." He stomped his feet. "It is *meant* to hang in the air by *magic*, or advanced alien technology, or *whatever* it is that keeps it from falling out of the sky. But it is not, I repeat, *not*—" he chopped his hand down into his open palm with each word "—Supposed. To. Have. A. Problem—" he sucked in more air "—With. My. Daughter. On. Board." He took several deep breaths and lowered his arms. He continued quietly, "I worry about my little girl enough without having *warning* lights, General."

Louise huffed and crossed her arms. "Mr. President, it's just a minor problem."

"I don't want *any* problems, Louise," shouted President Goodson, waving his fists in the air again.

General Greffen put up his open hands and spoke with a calm and even tone, like he was trying not to spook a skittish animal. "Mr. President, more than ninety-nine times out of a hundred, when a warning light comes on it just means that the sensor went bad. They checked your plane from stem to stern before they ever put it up in the air. The odds that there's really a problem with the nose gear hydraulics are ridiculous."

President Goodson sputtered wordlessly as images of plane crashes flitted past his mind's eye. "Nose gear hydraulics," he said. He wondered why all of the images had been in black and white, why many of them involved absurd airplanes with a dozen stacked wings collapsing under their own weight, and why the whole sequence ended with Slim Pickens riding on the bomb from Doctor Strangelove. He shook his head and rounded on Louise. "Nose gear hydraulics! Louise!"

"Mr. President, I—"

Just as suddenly, he twisted back toward General Greffen. His arms shot into the air, fingers splayed. "I want fighters in the air, General. I want a fighter escort for my daughter, you hear me?"

Louise continued in the same lecturing tone that would definitely not be calming him down. "Mr. President, that's really not necessary—"

"Mr. President, I understand why you're upset," said General Greffen. "I've got kids of my own, and they've certainly cost me plenty of sleep over the years. But this is just a minor problem. Just a light. Colonel Pritchard is one of the finest pilots in your Air Force, and he's not about to let anything go wrong up there. If he were worried about the airplane, he'd have called for an emergency landing. You've trusted him with your own life countless times, you know."

The president looked down at the conference table. He mumbled, "Well, that's different."

"You do trust him, don't you sir?"

President Goodson slowly lowered his arms, then let his shoulders slump. He nodded.

"Good," said General Greffen. "Let's let the man do his job, then. They'll be on the ground in three hours, and we'll all laugh about broken warning lights."

The president took a deep, shaky breath and let it out slowly. "You'd better be right, General."

General Greffen folded his arms and shot him a look that couldn't have said, 'oh really?' any more clearly.

A weak smile appeared on the president's lips. He stood up a little straighter and adjusted his tie.

"Magic, sir?" said General Greffen.

President Goodson raised an eyebrow at him.

"Or advanced alien technology?"

The president grinned. "Oh, don't you try to sell me that aerodynamics mumbo-jumbo, General. I've got the security clearance. I know how it really is."

General Greffen smiled. "Of course, sir."

"I'll want updates, General," the president said as he turned toward the door.

"Yes, Mr. President."

Chapter 29

SATURDAY

"If the cow knew what her hide was worth, would she be proud to be flayed?" tweeted Court. "Are we all just cattle to someone?" She shifted in her seat, the leather of the recliner creaking beneath her, and she dropped her phone into her lap. With her legs tucked up beneath her, the weight of the phone caused the lacy black hem of her dress to rise up and reveal a strip of skin above her thigh-high stockings. She sighed. Gawd, you'd think Air Force One wouldn't be so boring, but once you get past the burlwood and leather facade, you're still just stuck on an airplane, waiting to get on with things.

She let her eyes unfocus, trying to work up the energy to open her paperback again, which had turned out to suck—so far the vampire wasn't sparkly *at all*—when a naked girl in heels stomped past.

"Ta-da!" said Mandy, striking a fierce pose with her hands on her hips.

Court did a double-take. So, not quite naked, but close enough. Court would have felt embarrassed wearing that in the privacy of her own room, but Mandy really took the term 'shameless' to heart.

"Took you long enough," said Celeste, and darted past Mandy to the bathroom she'd just vacated.

Jessica, Britney and Harmony, sitting in leather recliners identical to Court's, looked up from their phones.

Jessica smirked. "You're changed already?"

"Ooh, maybe I should—" said Britney.

"It'll be hours yet before we land," said Jessica, shaking her head at Mandy, who had replaced her serious expression with a big grin. "And anyway, it's not like we'll be stepping off the plane and onto the beach."

Mandy folded her arms, which were covered with goosebumps. "But why waste any time?"

"She has a point," said Harmony.

Britney, who had ping-ponged from girl to girl with the conversation, stopped on Harmony, a confused smile on her face. "Who? Jessica or Mandy?"

Court couldn't take it anymore. She sighed hugely and said, "Oh, for god's sake, cover up. Look at you, you're freezing."

Mandy hugged her arms a little tighter about her, but said, "Sometimes one must make sacrifices—"

"I can't stand it!" said Court, whipping out her novel and attempting to block her view of the girls. "Even non-sparkly vampires are better than this."

"Alright, alright. Geez!" said Mandy. She stomped her way to an empty seat where she'd left her carry-on, her bare fake-tanned butt jiggling with each step.

Celeste flushed the airplane toilet, which loudly sucked up a swirl of blue liquid for a few seconds. She turned to the small sink and washed her hands, all the while making pouty lips and kissy lips and variations on smoldering come-hither looks in the mirror.

Above her head, a small round vent expelled a jet of cool air. And several thin insect legs. They scrabbled for purchase on the white plastic lip. Shortly thereafter, the legs were followed by the black and yellow head and torso of their owner. The tiny wasp struggled to pull itself through the narrow opening of the vent until suddenly it was ejected, tumbled in the stream of air, and caught itself a few inches away from the vent on the ceiling. It gnashed its mandibles and fluttered its wings with a few short high-pitched zings as it held fast to the ceiling.

Celeste cast a quick glance over her shoulder, shrugged and turned back to the mirror. She yawned at herself, then stretched her whole body—back arching, arms reaching above her head. "Mmmm," she mumbled as her fingers swiped within an inch of the bug.

The wasp dodged out of the way, dropping off the ceiling and hovering in the air with a whine.

Celeste spun around at the sound. Her hair whipped out, catching the flying insect and knocking it back into the door. She yelped when she saw it. After a split second's hesitation, she grabbed the door latch and yanked.

The door scissored into the crowded room and bounced off her foot, foiling her attempt to escape.

Still tumbling in the air, the wasp pinged off the door and then managed to right itself again. It zipped directly into Celeste's exposed cleavage.

She screamed and flailed.

It stung her.

She screamed louder and battered herself against the half-open door. She brushed frantically at her chest and somehow swept her attacker off her breast.

But it caught hold of her shirt, stinging her again through the material as she stumbled out of the restroom.

Celeste fell to the floor—eyes clinched shut and screaming her head off—and writhed spastically. Her hands swiped wildly over her clothes, flinging the wasp back into the bathroom.

Bhalsim guided the spray nozzle carefully back and forth across the wall of the barn, leaving behind a thin, sticky layer of foam that sealed the gaps between the wooden planks, nail holes and all manner of other small imperfections. He kept one hand on the metal spray tank at his side, to keep it from toppling over. Despite the relatively cool mid-day temp, his forehead glistened. His body armor trapped heat around him, and the tactical shotgun—stock folded and hanging limply at his chest—forced him to work just that much harder.

"How the hell did the colonel hear about this shit?" he said, knocking a knuckle against the canister and eliciting a hollow gong. "I've never heard of it."

A few yards away, Yonda was Bhalsim's stocky fraternal twin, spewing his own supply of foam onto the barn. He kept his eyes on the task, but said, "You watch football? Baseball?"

"Huh?"

"To relax. You watch sports?"

"Video games," said Bhalsim.

Yonda nodded slowly, then sidestepped to a portion of virgin wall. "Well, near as we can figure, the colonel reads. Spy novels, magazines of all sorts. And she files it all away in her head by tactical usefulness."

"And this jizz?"

Yonda snorted. "Damned if I know where she found it. But stick with us and you'll see some mighty interesting problem solving."

Bhalsim turned his attention back to the spraying. After a moment he said, "You like this out of the box thinking? Is that why you work for the colonel?"

Yonda cocked his head to the side and hesitated. "I guess that's a little of it. Sure."

"'Cause her busting my chops earlier—"

"Yeah," said Yonda, "she's got a wicked sense of humor. She's nailed most of us with something like that before. And it grows on you." He stopped spraying and looked around him, then balanced the spray wand on his tank. With a clattering of equipment and a grunt, he tried to shift a nearby crate closer to the wall.

Bhalsim set down his own sprayer and helped Yonda move the box. "You finish down low and I'll get up high?" he said after they'd repositioned the makeshift step-ladder.

Yonda grunted.

"That can't be all of it?" said Bhalsim after he'd resumed his task. "About the colonel."

"What do you want me to say?" Yonda sighed. "Look, I could tell you stories about the colonel single-handedly extracting the unit from insurgent strongholds, or staring down the brass when they'd give us a pointless objective, or balancing the safety of the unit with the success of the mission." Yonda stopped spraying and looked up at Bhalsim. "But you want to know if you can trust her command. That's gonna take watching what she does or making a leap of faith. Hell, maybe both. Anything I tell you is just—"

Fudley's hushed voice cut in on their earpieces. "I've got activity in the field behind the barn. Looks like some of the locals."

Beretta's voice responded, "Understood."

Yonda's sprayer hissed as he depressed the trigger again.

Bhalsim watched him, and then finally said, "Alright, I hear what you're—" The crack-crack of a pistol cut him off.

Immediately, Beretta's voice said, "Fudley report!" in their ears.

Bhalsim and Yonda simultaneously dropped their sprayers, and before the equipment could hit the ground, Beretta came back on the radio.

"Yonda, Bhalsim, converge on Fudley's position. All comms on vox. I need intel!"

Chapter 30

SATURDAY

Court had hardly found her place in the novel when Celeste's muffled shout pulled her back out. She dropped her book and leaned around the back of her seat to see down the aisle.

Celeste burst out of the bathroom, her hands waving frantically as she screamed. She tripped and fell to the floor.

Newly tank-topped and short-shorted—if you could even call them shorts—Mandy spun around. "Celeste! What happened?"

The other girls jumped from their seats and rushed toward Celeste.

"A wasp," gasped Celeste, crawling up the aisle toward her sisters. "In the bathroom."

Harmony hesitated and squeaked, "Help!"

Jessica and Mandy reached Celeste first, with Court nearly tripping over them as they dropped to the floor beside her. The girl's face was already blotchy, her breath ragged and wheezing.

Jessica shouted, "Somebody help us!"

Desmond and another Secret Service agent dashed onto the scene from further forward in the plane. He pushed Court and Mandy aside, taking a knee beside Jessica. "Reynolds, get the first aid kit," he shouted over his shoulder.

The other agent turned, yanked open a compartment in the wall and pulled out a blue box. In a few strides, he'd reached the knot of girls and thrust out the case. Jessica intercepted it as Desmond rolled Celeste onto her back.

He stared at the angry red welt blossoming on Celeste's breast. Then, after just a moment's hesitation, he tore open her shirt, exposing another hugely swollen lump on her side.

Jessica opened the first aid kit and Desmond snatched up an EpiPen. He popped the cover off with his thumb and jabbed it into Celeste's arm.

Almost immediately, Celeste's desperate gasping began to ease. She sucked in several wheezing breaths, like a weight had finally been lifted from her chest.

Harmony hung back, a white-knuckled fist closed over one of the seat backs. "Will she be ok?" she said.

Desmond let out a breath. "I think so," he said. "What the hell happened here?"

"She said it was a wasp," said Jessica.

Mandy added, "In the bathroom."

Celeste's hand closed around Desmond's and squeezed. He looked down at her and she smiled back at him.

"I'll always cherish this moment," she said weakly.

Court rolled her eyes and let out the breath she hadn't realized she'd been holding. Scaring her half to death and then still hitting on the hottie in the room! Really. And why was she even surprised?

Desmond returned the smile and then disentangled himself from Celeste's grasp. He stood, glanced about the space and snatched up a nearby magazine. As he made his way down the aisle, he rolled it tightly into a tube. When he reached the open door to the bathroom, he held the magazine in front of him like a fencer, hesitating an instant as he peered into the room, and then lunging and snapping it down onto the sink with a crack.

Desmond glanced around the bathroom more carefully. He frowned and swatted something on the ceiling, before reaching up and twisting the vent closed.

He came back up the aisle, saying to no one in particular, "There were two in there. Must be a nest somewhere." He knelt beside Celeste again. "Celeste, did you know you were allergic to wasps?"

Celeste shook her head gently. "I'm not allergic," she said quietly. "I've been stung before."

"Hmm," said Desmond.

"You don't think anyone else would go into shock like this, do you?" said Jessica.

"I don't know." Desmond gave the first aid kit an intense look. "But we aren't going to be able to treat many more people before we run out of supplies." He turned to the other agent. "Reynolds, arm yourself and keep an eye out for more wasps."

Reynolds reached hesitantly toward the sidearm holstered beneath his jacket. "Sir?" he said.

Desmond sighed. "You're on a plane full of sorority girls. Someone will loan you a magazine. I'll radio the ground and find out if there's something else we should be doing." Desmond stood and hurriedly exited toward the cockpit.

Harmony flexed her grip on the seatback, the leather squeaking and popping under her hand. "I can't believe this is happening," she said finally.

Britney peeked her head over Harmony's shoulder, surveying the damage. "I know," she said, shaking her head. "That top was *so* cute on her."

"Maybe we can find another one," said Mandy.

Harmony nodded.

"No," said Britney. "It's from last year's collection."

Mandy, Britney and Harmony all sighed.

"At last report, the rescued hostages were being assessed at a secure medical facility," said General Greffen. "All those deemed fit for travel will be on a plane out of Julala by this evening, Mr. President." He dropped the agenda on top of the stack of papers cluttering the Situation Room conference table and looked up at the president.

President Goodson was leaned back in his chair, with his weight shifted off to one side, and his legs crossed. He nodded slowly, a studious expression on his face.

Greffen sat back and clasped his hands in front of him. He'd finally gotten a halfway decent night's sleep last night, now that the hostage crisis was resolved, but he was still tired. He was actually looking forward to more regular old mundane briefings like this one. About the only thing still in the way of that was the damned bug—

Louise McCracken cleared her throat. "That's it then, General?"

But there *was* the matter of that damned bug. He hadn't added it to the agenda. Momma hadn't raised her boy to pass the buck. But the last thing he wanted was for the story to break before he told the president. If Stuart was right, this particular experimental atrocity run amuck would soon be awfully hard to miss. "Well—"

"I've been spending too much time in here, General," said President Goodson. "I'm thinking about having my desk moved down from the Oval Office. It'll save me time running back and forth, don't you think?"

Ah, hell, he could give his team a few more hours before he troubled the president with it. "There's nothing else—"

One of Greffen's aids dashed to his side. "General Greffen, sir. Agent Franks from Air Force One is on the radio. He's saying something about an allergic reaction to a wasp sting."

President Goodson sent his chair tumbling backward as he leapt to his feet. "That's it, General. That's the last straw." He leaned over the table and stabbed at it with his finger. "I want fighters in the air! I want that plane on the ground and I want my baby girl back here right now!"

The shocked look on McCracken's face quickly became stern. "Mr. President, you're over-reacting," she said. "We hardly need to send up fighters over some insects."

"Send Dr. Rhys-Billingsly over here, soldier," said General Greffen.

"I am the President of these United States. Commander-in-Chief. When I say I want a damned fighter escort, I should get a damned fighter escort."

McCracken stood up. "Mr. President! Think of the taxpayer expense. Over a bug. It's a gross misuse of resources."

Greffen's aid reappeared with Stuart in tow, and Greffen turned his attention away from the president and McCracken. "Stuart. Stuart!" Greffen snapped his fingers in front of Stuart's awestruck face.

"Hmm?" said Stuart. He looked away from the arguing president and chief of staff. "Yeah?"

"We've got wasps on Air Force One. Could it be related?"

Stuart frowned and then shrugged. "Possibly? Not enough data, George."

Greffen turned back to his aid. "I want a fighter escort on Air Force One yesterday, soldier!"

"Sir!"

McCracken was incredulous. "General!"

President Goodson folded his arms and looked smug.

"I've never much liked coincidences, Louise," said Greffen.

The president looked a bit less certain.

"Louise, Mr. President, I'd like you to meet my friend Dr. Stuart Rhys-Billingsly." Greffen suggested they all sit with a wave of his hand. "I believe there's one more item that bears discussion."

Chapter 31

SATURDAY

Fudley felt like he'd been hit in the chest with a sledge hammer. White sprites zig-zagged over top of that paunchy, gap-toothed redneck motherfucker that had shot him. He studied that smug look, the silver 1911 still leveled at his chest, the other denim and flannel wearing locals emerging from the almond orchard, during the eon it took him to stagger backward.

From some distance down a well, he heard Beretta say, "Fudley report," whatever the hell that meant.

The little drill sergeant in the back of his mind said, point your gun and shoot this motherfucker. Oh, and breathing would be a good idea, too, soldier.

His arms knew when to follow orders, even if his lungs didn't. And that's when Fudley noticed the pain. It was a stabbing pain, a searing pain, a white-hot lance of agony that completely overruled earlier directives, and drowned out the chipmunk chattering in his ear. Fudley wondered how he'd managed to notice anything else, ever. And then he wondered how he was wondering when there was *so much pain* he could be paying attention to instead.

Fortunately, the drill sergeant was not concerned about pain. What didn't kill you, and all that inspirational bullshit, soldier. No, the sergeant saw those other rednecks raising up their rifles toward Fudley. And he said, soldier, you will eat the dirt *and you will like it*.

The ground was a damn fine recruit, followed orders like a professional, and promptly smacked Fudley right in the chin. Fudley gasped, sucking in as much dust as air, and the world around him suddenly accelerated. The enemy dashed past him and disappeared into the barn. He coughed and felt Yonda's huge mitt clap down on his back. Bhalsim was suddenly crouched beside him, weapon trained on the orchard.

"Got him," said Yonda.

"Fall back," said Bhalsim.

A pop sounded somewhere out amongst the almond blossoms, and a puff of dust appeared beside the trio.

"Taking fire from the almond orchard," grumbled Bhalsim. He returned fire with a boom-rip, boom-rip as the shotgun pellets tore into the trees.

As Yonda dragged him backward, Fudley finally started to shift his thoughts away from the pain in his arm. He managed to crawl along with Yonda, or, at least, not offer quite so much resistance to the freight locomotive with a grip on his vest. And the words twittering in his earpiece stopped sounding quite so much like gibberish.

Beretta's voice cut in, "Yonda, bring Fudley to point alpha. Bhalsim, find cover and watch those trees."

Fudley coughed again, and then wheezed, "Barn is compromised. Multiple hostiles."

"Shit," said Beretta. "Everyone rendezvous at alpha."

"He'll have a cracked rib or two," growled Luile. "But the vest stopped the bullets."

Beretta peered down at Fudley over Luile's shoulder. With Yonda and Bhalsim watching the barn, she could focus on Fudley. Her palms were sweating, and she kept sliding them over the grips of her pistols. "And the arm?"

"It's fucked up," he said.

"Is that your professional opinion?" She squeezed the pistols, but kept her voice flat.

"Textbook case, ma'am."

Keeping his eyes closed, Fudley hissed through clenched teeth, "I'm good, Colonel. Got another arm."

"Sorry, Fud. You're sidelined unless this op goes totally south. Then you come save our butts one-handed."

Fudley started to chuckle, and then quickly transitioned into a groan. He nodded.

"Alright." Beretta released her pistols and folded her arms. "Give me the play-by-play. What the hell happened?"

"Was watching the barn, not my back. This is fucking—" Fudley grimaced "—America." He took a slow breath. "Motherfucker got the drop on me."

"How many made it inside?"

Fudley shook his head very carefully. "Three. Four. Not sure."

Beretta turned back toward the barn. She and Luile had managed to seal the hayloft window. The rest of the building was maybe half slimed, but that made little difference with a redneck wildcard hanging out inside. Well, Plan A was out.

She had Plan B sitting in the SUV. She would have preferred not to use it. Too messy. And to be effective, she'd need to deploy it inside the barn, which brought her back around to her redneck problem.

Pretty much any which way she sliced it, the first thing she needed to do was neutralize their unwanted guests. Who were armed and hiding in a building full of unpredictable killer mutant wasps. While an unknown number of snipers hid in the surrounding orchards.

She smiled. Yup, just another typical Saturday.

Chapter 32

SATURDAY

President Goodson drew in a slow, deep breath as he held the bridge of his nose in his fingers. He'd closed his eyes to the bustle of activity in the Situation Room, but he could feel the others' expectant gazes on him. The most important thing was to keep his mind on the big picture, and not— Whoa, close one there. Big picture. He released his breath and looked at General Greffen. "Alright, General, let me make sure I've got this right. There's a *giant mutant wasp* running amok somewhere in my country—" he ticked the points off on his fingers "—one known fatality, a wet team—"

Louise cut in, "Precision strike team."

"—precision strike team—thank you, Louise—preparing to hit a suspected *nest of mutant wasps*, and one of my daughter's friends—" he cleared his throat "—

has just been stung by a wasp, *that may also be a mutant*, on Air Force One." Big picture. *Big picture.*

"Yes, sir, that pretty well sums it up," said Greffen.

"And I'm only hearing about all this *now!?*"

"Well, Mr. President, it just hadn't escalated to a point where you needed to be informed."

President Goodson shook his head. "Sometimes it just doesn't pay to be the leader of the free world." He couldn't even tell himself this was the strangest security briefing he'd ever had. Probably the most personal— *big picture!* And look at Louise jotting notes on her legal pad. Tell her there's a rampaging genetic abomination terrorizing the populace and the first thing on her mind is controlling the news cycle if it leaks. He tried to catch a glimpse of her chicken scratches, but the old-school shorthand was indecipherable. Bet she's already got ideas about how to leverage this to pick up more of the hippie anti-GMO vote in the next campaign cycle.

Louise stopped scribbling and said, "What do we know for certain about this mutant wasp, General?"

Greffen turned to the scientist he'd brought to the table. "Stuart?"

Doctor Rhys-Billingsly looked nervous. Under other circumstances, the president would have tried to make him feel at ease. But with his daughter— today, the soft touch was not a priority.

"Well," said Rhys-Billingsly, "the *Sceliphron caementarium* is a fierce hunter and actually fills a crucial role in pest management because of the parasitic nature of its life cycle. Though, actually, this specimen is a hybridization with the *Vespa mandarinia*—a tricky endeavor, if I do say so myself, that took me a couple of years to achieve—"

"Stuart," said Greffen, "why don't you just give us the executive summary?"

"Oh. Er, right." Rhys-Billingsly didn't seem to know what to do with his hands, and began to gesture randomly as he spoke. "So, we know that it's growing at an unprecedented rate. If my figures are accurate—and I've been over them and over them, got the decimals in all the right places—"

"Stuart."

Rhys-Billingsly blanched. "Er, the wasp could easily be the size of a truck at this point. And, um, its sting also appears to be unusually potent. I was stung just moments after exposing it to the mutagen and I've had a severe reaction."

Wait. Exposing it to the mutagen? *This guy* created this monster? A twinge in his jaw caused President Goodson to realize he'd been grinding his teeth and fantasizing about all manner of terrible things he'd do to the man if— he focused back on Rhys-Billingsly's rambling.

"—if the nest Colonel Beretta has found is indeed related to the original wasp, then it's exhibiting extremely strange reproductive behavior. There's no telling what other effects the mutation has had on the wasp, or what it might pass on to its offspring."

The president clasped his hands on the table, his knuckles white as he struggled to contain himself. Rather quietly, he said, "Were there other subjects, Doctor? Other wasps?"

"Hmm? Oh, yes, certainly."

"And what happened to them?"

Rhys-Billingsly shrugged. "I don't know. I was reassigned."

President Goodson turned a loaded look on General Greffen.

"We've tried, sir," said Greffen, "but it's Ransom Research Corporation. They've stonewalled, and my team tells me that we don't have a legal leg to stand on. All of the regulatory bodies signed off on the research."

"Regulatory compliance isn't my area," said Rhys-Billingsly, "but I know we use a top-notch consultant. Some Lawyer and his group, I think."

Greffen grumbled, "It's always the damned lawyers, sir."

"Actually," said Rhys-Billingsly, but he wilted under the president's glare. "Er, nevermind," he mumbled.

"So, General," said the president, "where's the wasp now?"

Greffen sighed. "We're not exactly certain, Mr. President."

President Goodson shook his head. "Wasp the size of a bus, and you—"

Louise looked up from her notes. "At least we've got the barn contained, Mr. President."

The president sat back as one of Greffen's aids rushed to his side. "Excuse me, General. I've got Colonel Beretta on the line."

"Put her through on the speaker," said Greffen.

The aid pressed a few buttons and the speaker hissed to life. Greffen announced himself.

Colonel Beretta's irritated voice cut on."We've had a complication, General."

President Goodson sighed.

Greffen leaned in toward the phone and barked, "Out with it, Colonel."

"Some local yahoos shot one of my boys and breached the barn."

"And the nest?" said Greffen.

"Still contained, General."

Louise dropped her pen on her pad. "Brilliant. I bet they voted Republican, too."

Chapter 33

SATURDAY

Dwayne and Owen leaned hard on the main sliding door of the barn, which slammed home with a dull boom. Woodrow and Roy lowered the weapons they had trained on the door and the four men put a little distance between themselves and the entry. They shared a nervous look with each other and then Roy hunched and panted heavily from the sprint into the barn.

A couple hollow pops sounded outside, followed by some big booms, and as one, the militiamen cringed. Then there was silence.

Woodrow almost giggled, but bit his lip instead. He wiped one sweaty hand on his jeans, before squeezing the forestock of his rifle to hide the tremor in his hand. He glanced around the barn, trying to pick out the details in the unusually dark space. The efforts the soldiers had made to seal the barn had effectively choked out most of the natural light leaks. Almost all of the available light filtered in through a handful of bullet holes in the sliding door and wall. Was that from the covering fire Roy had demanded? Woodrow tried not to think too hard about the fact that this meant he was currently downrange of his compatriots, who could not possibly see him through the wall of the barn. His worries must be unfounded, as Roy and the others paid no mind to the bullet holes and grinned at each other nervously.

"That's right, boys," said Roy, between gulps of air. "No government types can step on us, no sir."

"No sir!" said Dwayne.

Woodrow nodded a little too enthusiastically and said, "That's right!"

"This here barn is ours and we gonna keep it," continued Roy. He glanced around the barn, and then pointed at Dwayne and Owen. "Dwayne, Owen, you tuck yourselves out of the way and watch them doors."

Roy made a vaguely military gesture that looked pretty cool to Woodrow, even if he hadn't the slightest idea what it was supposed to mean.

"Woodrow, you and me, we'll get up in the loft and hold the high ground."

Woodrow nodded appreciatively. "Gotta take the high ground, eh, Roy?" He was pretty sure he'd heard plenty of military types in the movies talking about high ground. And being an extra story above the line of fire seemed like a better idea than hanging out in front of the door.

"Damn straight," said Roy. Still breathing hard, he eyed the ladder up to the loft for half a second. He turned back to the men. "Boys, we done an important thing today. We showed them government types they can't push us around none. We showed 'em that it's power *of* the people, *by* the people, and *for* the people. We can't let 'em do to us what they done to ol' Darryl."

Owen shook his head. "Damn shame about ol' Darryl."

"Amen," said Dwayne.

Roy looked wearily at the ladder again. "Alright, hop to it boys," he said. He holstered his pistol and mounted the first rung.

He climbed rather more slowly than Woodrow would have preferred, grunting quietly every step or so. When he was finally hauling himself into the loft, Woodrow spryly ascended behind him.

Roy shuffled around in the dusty loft, staying almost prone and quite near to the ladder. He sneezed a few times, and then, seeing Woodrow framed in the loft opening, waved emphatically at him.

Woodrow mutely pointed at himself and then further back into the loft. He decided to interpret Roy's increasingly agitated waving as a yes, and moved back away from the entrance. He crouched and shouldered his rifle, establishing that he had terrible sightlines on anywhere there might be action. After a moment's consideration, Woodrow decided this was probably for the best, anyway. He tried his hand at a half-remembered military-movie-gesture, but Roy was facing the other way and half obscured by a pile of loose hay. That, actually, came as some relief, since he was pretty sure he just looked stupid gesticulating like that.

Chapter 34

SATURDAY

Captain Hubert Dane squinted into the bright blue sky that surrounded the bubble canopy of his F-35 Lightning fighter jet. In the distance, the horizon curved noticeably and wispy white clouds created a mottled floor that obscured much of the Earth below. Air Force One was still too far out to make visual. He glanced over his shoulder—the mask dangling by one strap from his helmet swinging awkwardly—and confirmed the position of his wingman in formation behind him. He turned forward again.

"Control, this is Lightning One. I have Air Force One on radar. Intercept in thirty seconds."

"Understood, Lightning One," crackled in his ear.

Hubert reached out and stroked the side of the photo he'd wedged amongst the instrumentation. Just how many aircraft would the Air Force have to commission before someone made a photo frame a standard part of the cockpit? As it was, the F-35 was packed so tightly that Hubert's picture obscured part of the primary display.

But, squee! So worth it. Captain Pugslington, his dog, looked *so cute* in his itsy-bitsy bomber jacket and helmet. And he'd been so excited to do that photo shoot, *yes he had*. What a good boy. And just as soon as Daddy finished babysitting silly old Air Force One, he'd go home and give him so many kisses. Would Captain Pugslington like that? *Yes he would.*

A shiny speck on the horizon rapidly expanded into the gleaming Air Force One, apparently hanging solidly in the empty space ahead. Hubert toggled his mic and, in a clipped and stoic tone, said, "Control, Lightning One. We have visual on Air Force One. There appears to be something dangling from the fuselage." He leaned forward against the harness crossing his chest, as though the extra centimeter would improve the view. "Holiest of the shit— Lightning two, are you seeing this?"

With nearly the same flat disinterest, Lightning Two responded in his ear, "Affirmative, Lightning One. I cannot believe my eyes. The shit is truly holy."

"Be advised, Control," said Hubert, "there is an enormous fucking wasp hanging onto Air Force One."

"What the hell does that thing want?" demanded President Goodson. He clenched and released his fists over and over as he squinted at Doctor Rhys-Billingsly.

He'd swear he'd heard the man counting under his breath, and at the moment, the doctor looked a little too disconnected for the president's liking.

Louise emphatically jabbed her pen against her notepad. "We don't negotiate with mutant wasps, Mr. President."

"And why the hell is it on my airplane?"

After an intense few seconds of looking like a startled deer caught in the president's dazzling glare, President Goodson watched Rhys-Billingsly's face relax and his eyes glaze over. With the sort of monotone that has lulled countless college students to sleep, he began to lecture, "Actually, Mr. President—"

Fantastic. His daughter's life is on the line and Greffen brings him the absent-fucking-minded professor. And then Louise—

"At least you're not up there, too, Mr. President."

He looked at her and fumed as Rhys-Billingsly's monotone lapped at the shores of his understanding.

"—this behavior is similar to—"

Louise was making an artform out of *not getting it*. Would it come as a surprise to *anyone* that she'd never had kids?

"—wasps of the family Pompilidae—"

Enough. "Look, I don't care what it takes, we've got to protect my baby girl."

"—are known as Spider Wasps—"

Greffen sighed. "Mr. President, believe me when I say I want to bring that plane home safe and sound."

"—they paralyze a spider and then—"

Greffen continued, "Our priority has to be destroying that wasp. There's no telling what could happen if it should escape."

"—lay their eggs inside it—"

Louise spit the words out first. "Those fighters can't attack as long as Air Force One is in the way."

You're damned right they can't.

"—when the eggs hatch—"

Louise continued, "Just think of the taxpayer expense of replacing that airplane."

The president slapped his hand over his eyes in frustration.

"—the offspring eat the spider from the inside out."

The sudden absence of Rhys-Billingsly's monotone was just enough to derail the rant ready to burst out of the president. He played back the last thing he'd heard in his mind and threw up his hands against further interruption. "Wait," he said. "Doctor, are you saying the wasps inside Air Force One are going to *eat* the people on board?"

Rhys-Billingsly seemed to drop out of his trance and rejoin the president at the table. "Hmm? Oh, well, I don't know. But there's certainly precedent for that sort of behavior. And many wasps are meat eaters."

"I want that plane on the ground now, General." President Goodson jabbed his finger onto the table.

"Mr. President," said Greffen with careful restraint, "we need to engage that wasp. If we wait until Air Force One is on the ground, the fighters will be useless."

"Say, George?" said Rhys-Billingsly, a thoughtful frown on his face. "How good are your pilots?"

Greffen kept his eyes locked with the president. "The best. Why?"

"Well, considering the typical behaviors of the Pomp—"

"Stuart!"

Rhys-Billingsly flinched. "It'll defend Air Force One. If the wasp sees the fighters as a threat, it'll defend Air Force One."

Everyone looked at Rhys-Billingsly.

President Goodson said, "It'll let go of the plane?"

Rhys-Billingsly nodded. "Yeah. It would have to."

Greffen made a grim smile. "That would give my fighters a chance to take it out."

"Give the order, General."

Louise stopped her pen and said, "And what do we do about the wasps *inside* Air Force One?"

Rhys-Billingsly piped up again. "They'd probably be susceptible to—"

President Goodson growled, "We'll worry about that later. Make the move, General!"

"Yes, sir!"

Louise scribbled furiously in her notes, saying, "Just don't blow up the plane, General. You know the Republicans would nail us during the campaign." She glanced up at the ensuing silence. "What?"

Chapter 35

SATURDAY

"The wasp more than likely knocked out the nose gear hydraulics when it reached the plane," said General Greffen's voice, tinny and even rougher around the edges thanks to the radio system.

Desmond held one can of the headset up to his ear as he stood in front of the radio console. He nodded at Colonel Pritchard, who sat beside him with his own headset properly covering both ears.

"Affirmative, General," said Pritchard. "We'll lower the gear manually."

"You have your orders, gentlemen," said Greffen, his statement punctuated with a pop of static.

"Yes, sir," both men replied at once.

Pritchard pulled this headset down around his neck and yanked the plug out of the radio console.

"We'll leave the landing gear to you and your man, Agent Franks."

"Yes, sir." Desmond set the headset beside the console.

"You can access the manual nose gear release in the forward cargo hold."

"Understood, sir."

"You're familiar with the access routes?" said Pritchard.

Desmond nodded.

"Good." Pritchard hesitated for a moment, and then sighed. "I hate to say this, Agent Franks, but odds are good those wasps were coming from the cargo hold."

Desmond picked up the curled magazine that he'd left on the desktop beside him. He fixed it with a determined glare as he twisted it into a tight roll. "Don't worry, Colonel," he said. "We'll be ready."

Colonel Pritchard stood and thrust out his hand.

Desmond met his eyes and shook his hand firmly, then he turned and made his way back to the passenger cabin.

Court perched on the edge of her seat, holding her phone tightly to keep her hands from trembling. Which was ridiculous, because it's not as though she needed to be freaked out, or anything. Celeste's encounter with a wasp was just a freak thing. Startling, for sure, but nothing that should justify this aching worry in the pit of her stomach. And anyway, Desmond killed the thing.

Crisis averted, right? It's not like there's some menacing, Hitchcockian swarm, just waiting to burst in.

She suppressed a shudder and looked over at Celeste, who was settled back on one of the recliners, pale but breathing normally. Jessica and Mandy hovered around her, while Agent Reynolds watched stoically from further up the aisle. Britney and Harmony had retreated back to their seats moments before, their usual vacant expressions tinged with anxiety.

Desmond strode in from the front of the plane. He clasped his hands together and said, "Alright, ladies, we're going to make an emergency landing soon, so I need everybody buckled in." He turned to Agent Reynolds before any of the girls could articulate their surprise. "Head back and get the rest of the girls settled. Then gather together as many magazines as you can."

Reynolds nodded once and headed down the aisle.

"And find me some duct tape," Desmond called at his back.

The term 'emergency landing' escalated Court's nerves from a few butterflies to full-blown-climbing-up-her-throat-in-glorious-technicolor nausea. Was Celeste dying? Were they all going to die? If they were about to die, should she be live tweeting it?

She had just caught up to the mystery of the duct tape when Desmond took a knee beside Celeste's seat.

"How's the patient?" he said to Celeste with a smile.

Celeste peered at him through half closed eyes and said quietly, "You can tear open my shirt again and have a look. Go on, I don't mind."

Mandy chuckled. "Seems like she's doing just fine," she said and moved off to settle on her own recliner.

Jessica turned to Desmond, the worry in her voice clear. "She's not so bad we need to make an emergency landing, is she?"

Before Desmond could answer, Celeste said in a husky whisper, "I mean it, Desmond. You should have another look. Look at whatever you like."

If Court hadn't already been fighting to keep her stomach under control, that response would have made her want to hurl. Gawd, that girl had a one track mind.

Desmond and Jessica shared a little smile and then he gave Celeste a squeeze on the shoulder. "Buckle-up, ladies. We'll be on the ground in a minute," he said.

Agent Reynolds barreled down the aisle, hefting a stack of magazines topped with a roll of duct tape. Desmond indicated at a side table with a nod of his head, and Reynolds dumped the pile atop it with a thud.

Desmond grabbed the tape and a couple of magazines, holding one out to Reynolds. "Tear that one apart, Reynolds," he said.

Britney gasped. "Not the Fall Fashion Preview! I haven't finished it yet," she whined.

"Oh my god," said Mandy, "there's the cutest sweater on page 87. It's *so* you!"

"Oh! Save me that page, save me that page!"

Reynolds made quick work of the magazine, rapidly tearing it down into a pile of loose pages while Desmond did the same to his own.

Mandy leaned forward and pointed urgently. "There. There it is."

Reynolds glanced at Desmond. Unlike Court, he didn't roll his eyes, but he sighed as he fished the page out of the pile and handed it over to Harmony.

"Oh. My. God!" said Harmony.

Mandy nodded. "I know, right?"

Court clapped her hand over her eyes in disgust.

Meanwhile, Desmond began laying out the pages and taping them into a large sheet.

Chapter 36

SATURDAY

By rights, Beretta should have been extremely annoyed. Despite the fact that barns full of mutant wasps did not figure into her average weekend, the whole op had been running practically on rails. Until rednecks showed up, shot her boy and generally FUBARed the day. Yeah, she should be pissed, but as she ghosted through the orchard, she couldn't help but grin hugely.

With an M9 in one hand and a taser in the other, she moved amongst the trees so silently that the birds and crickets hadn't noticed, continuing to chirp without a care in the world. When their song finally did taper off, she knew she was nearly on top of the pair of snipers she'd come out here to neutralize.

"Lookit, Jimmy. They shot me!"

She stopped.

"They din't shoot you, Zach," grumbled Jimmy in response.

"They did!" said Zach. "Lookit, it broke the skin an' everythin'."

Beretta crept closer until she could properly see the pair. The younger of the two was crouched by a tree and cradling his hand, his weapon lying on the ground a few feet away.

"There's blood, see," continued Zach. He held his hands out toward Jimmy, but Jimmy didn't look.

Jimmy lay prone, staring intensely over his iron sites at the barn. "I saw the firs' time," he said. "I don't need to see it a hunert times more. Y'ain't shot. 's just a shotgun pellet. Idjit gover'ment soldiers. Who the hell uses shotguns to defend their base?"

No, she wasn't even peeved. She took pride in the missions that went off without a hitch. But they were just so *dull*. Sometimes, she really needed to get out and stretch a little. Keep the skills sharp. Solve a few puzzles. Maybe get a little cardio in, since she'd missed some of her regular gym time.

Yonda would probably be in position by now. She'd sent him to deal with another pair of snipers while Luile and Bhalsim looked after Fudley and the barn. She clicked her radio twice. A second later she heard two clicks in her earpiece. Go time! She sent one more ping back on the radio and, with a long silent stride, closed the distance to the good ol' boys. She leapt into the air and landed on Jimmy's back with a crunch and an electric tack-tack-tack-tack.

Beretta smiled at Zach, who stared back at her with his mouth gaping open. She stopped zapping Jimmy and all of the knotted muscles beneath her turned to mush.

Zach blinked slowly and then reached for his rifle.

Beretta pointed her M9 at his face and said, "uh uh uh."

His hand trembled but halted. A wet spot blossomed on his pants.

"Zach," she said. "I think we should have a chat."

Louise McCracken sat back in her chair. "Really? Bug spray?"

Stuart Rhys-Billingsly shrugged. "Well, I mean, size notwithstanding, they are just wasps, after all."

General Greffen flipped slowly through the stack of reconnaissance photos sent back by his fighter jets. He just couldn't force his mind to see the wasp as an enormous monster grasping the underside of Air Force One. Instead, he saw a bug hugging a teeny toy plane. But big or small, the wasp made him want to cringe. After all these decades, his nemesis had returned.

"Fine," said President Goodson. "We'll get everyone out and hose down the plane, then."

Greffen shook off the memory of sweltering summer heat, buzzing insects, and crushing life lessons. He turned to one of his men and said, "You heard the president, soldier. I want exterminators and wasp killer waiting for that plane."

"We'll never get the smell out of the upholstery," mumbled McCracken, shaking her head.

"And the barn?" said the president.

Greffen pointed at another soldier. "You! Pesticide to Colonel Beretta. Figure it out." He turned back to the president. "I'm sure that'll be useful, but it won't get to her fast enough."

"Then what are our options?"

"Don't worry about Beretta, Mr. President," said Greffen. "She's a problem solver."

President Goodson nodded. "Fair enough. We're clear, then?"

General Greffen grunted.

"Make it happen, General."

Greffen stood, looking down at the photos again, recalling the oppressive humidity and stagnant air from that day in his youth. The painful memory, like fire, swept through his mind's eye. He felt the burn of it on his face. Heard the squeek-thunk of the back door closing, and the drone of cicadas hidden somewhere amongst the vibrant growth of the yard. And then the ominous buzzing from behind, a harbinger he'd been heedless of that fateful day. He turned his eyes to the ceiling of the Situation Room, but saw only what played back in his mind. "Mr. President, when I was a boy of about ten, I lived in a big old house that backed up on some acreage. For a boy, all that greenery and space became my kingdom, or the fields of battle, or the thickest of jungles concealing lost civilizations. The possibilities seemed endless and I was the invincible conqueror of it all. Until one day." He closed his eyes. "A monster came swooping down out of the deepest of the eaves of that old house, like a raptor hunting its prey. A wasp!" He shuddered. "It practically knocked me to the ground, and without the slightest provocation, stung me just above my eye. I can feel the searing pain of it even now. My face was swollen for a week, but the damage lasted longer than that. It stole my innocence, sir. Made me doubt my own immortality." He looked down at Stuart. "Dare I say it, Stuart, but that wasp made us the men we are today." He shook his head and raised a fist into the air. "Well, Mr. President, it's payback time!" He slammed his fist onto the table. "Operation: BLACKFLAG is go!"

Chapter 37

SATURDAY

Wasp-self clung to the underside of the shiny non-wasp creature, pressing her body tightly against it. The wind whistling past her abdomen tickled her wings. She shivered with ecstasy. Holding the source of that intoxicating aroma so close, feeling the exhaustion from the hard-won flight, sinking her stinger deep into its belly—she'd never felt such satisfaction in all her life. How long had she been hanging here? It didn't matter. Perhaps in a little bit, she'd sting it again. But for now she'd wait, let the *antennae-waggling* anticipation build.

And yet! The infuriating non-wasp creature continued to fly! Cold wind continued to whip at Wasp-self's body! Rage burbled up within her, balancing out the joy. Did the creature not understand that it should be screaming in agony, falling to the ground, struggling and failing to move? How could it continue on, as though its guts were not already sustenance for the wasp-offspring?

A dark shaped moved below her, distracting her from the insolence of the shiny non-wasp. What dared to move in her presence? She twitched her head. *The flexing of her forelegs*, there were *two* of them! Two, dark non-wasps, flying in her presence. The nerve of these creatures! How long had they been there? Were they after her prey?!

One of the pursuers suddenly streaked past her, hissing horribly.

Her body bounced in the wake of its passing, her grip slipping minutely. This— This was incomprehensible! The silver creature was *her* prey! It would feed *her* offspring!! How dare these usurpers bother her?!!! She would have vengeance!!!!

How was that, Captain Pugslington, *hmm?* Did Daddy buzz Air Force One like a badass? *Yes he did!*

"Break right, Lightning One."

Captain Hubert Dane sucked in a breath of the cold air hissing into his mask, tweaked the stick in his hand, and grunted as his body weight quintupled. He'd reacted to his wingman's advice with pure, battle-hardened instinct, and his conscious thoughts scrambled under the sudden g's. In his mind's eye, he saw Captain Pugslington behind the controls of an F-35, flight goggles over his eyes and long white scarf whipping in the wind.

"The wasp is hot on your six," said Captain Pugslington lazily. "Manoeuvre alpha."

Hubert executed the manoeuvre, just like Captain Pugslington—no, Lightning Two—had said, rolling the jet out of the turn and performing a tight loop. He hicked and hurked his way through the increasing g's, flexing his muscles to keep from graying out. He couldn't see the enemy, a potentially deadly complication that tempted him to swivel his head around. But with his body under this much pressure, it was all he could do to keep looking forward. He'd have to trust his wingman.

"Gamma, gamma, gamma," drawled Lightning Two in Hubert's ear.

He yanked the throttle back, which felt just about like the mid-air equivalent to standing on the anti-lock brakes, and arced the aircraft into a barrel roll. Where the hell was that damned wasp?!

A massive black and yellow shape shot in front of him, then stopped. "Shit." Hubert yanked back on the stick, slammed the throttle forward and peeled off course. "Bogey stops on a dime."

"Roger that, Lightning One. I overshot and lost visual."

Hubert brought the plane around, forced to rely on his instruments to know which way was up. Blips for his wingman and the retreating Air Force One winked at him on the radar screen. But no sign of the wasp. Had it ever showed up? He leveled off before he caught sight of the insect, a mere speck in the distance. Was it— "Bogey has turned to pursue Air Force One." With a flick of his thumb, he engaged the targeting computer. Come on, come on, you multi-million-dollar piece of crap.

The computer patiently waited for Hubert to line up on a hostile aircraft while the speck of a wasp rapidly expanded to fill the view.

"I can't get a lock," said Hubert. Could he use the guns? He had no idea where the bullets would land. "Permission to switch to guns, Command?" Maybe on the next run—

"This is Lightning Two. I've regained visual on—holy shit!"

The wasp zigged and spun in the air unlike any aircraft Hubert had ever seen. With blurring speed and deft precision, it grappled his plane as he tried to veer away. More alarms blared and lights lit than he thought were even on this bird.

"Eject, eject, eject!" shouted Lightning Two.

Hubert grabbed the handles above his head and heaved on them. With a resounding crack, the canopy blasted away somewhere behind him, and then he felt like his cheeks pooled in his lap as he rocketed into the open air.

Agent Desmond Franks tore the duct tape with his teeth, then slapped the strip amongst the others dangling from Agent Reynold's suit jacket. "Are we clear?" he said.

"Yes sir."

Desmond turned back toward the hatch in the floor, but hesitated. He ripped off one more piece of tape, searching for a moment for an open spot on his own suit to stick it. He dropped to one knee and nodded, mostly to himself. "Here goes nothing," he said. He pulled the latch and opened the entry into the cargo hold.

He couldn't see any immediate threats in the weak, yellow light down below, so he dropped the roll of tape and a few magazines into the open space and climbed down the ladder.

A big bundle of luggage hemmed Desmond in on one side, leaving only a narrow path forward. He pulled the rolled up magazine from his inside coat pocket and twisted it tighter as he looked for any sign of hostile activity ahead. The wasp he'd killed earlier had been small. Small enough to miss. But if Celeste's reaction was any indication, one sting might be enough to incapacitate him. And if he should fail in his mission— no, it didn't bear thinking about. He couldn't fail. Not now. Not ever again!

Something brushed against his head and he instinctively ducked and raised the magazine like a sword. But it was just Reynolds, waving the folded bunch of pages that they had taped together earlier. Desmond grabbed it, then retrieved the tape and magazines from the floor. As soon as he was clear of the ladder, Reynolds joined him.

The path forward was too narrow for them to walk abreast. Desmond would have to take point until they got clear of the luggage. Wordlessly, he handed the sheet and the extra magazines to Reynolds, then crept forward with his weapon raised.

He kept his breathing slow and steady, calling on his years of training to control the urge to flee, to harness the adrenaline and use it to hone his senses. This wasn't like last time. And he wasn't the same agent now as he was back then. He was prepared to die to accomplish this mission. But how did the saying go? Don't die for your mission; make the enemy die for his. He'd come too far, worked too hard to die in the line of duty. That's right! Today he'd *kill* in the line of duty. He'd squish 'em. Squish 'em all with his bare hands, if he had to.

Ten agonizing feet later, the luggage ended and things got a wee bit roomier. Their goal was centered in the floor ahead of them: the manual nose gear controls. And hardly three feet beyond that was something— something wrong. Organic. Seemingly erupting out of the floor. And absolutely squirming with tiny black and yellow creatures.

"Shit," whispered Reynolds.

Desmond grabbed one corner of the sheet Reynolds was holding. "Let's do this!" he said.

Crouching in the dark, staring at a small patch of dirty barn floor visible over the edge of the hayloft, Woodrow found the sudden calm strangely peaceful. He could hear little besides his own rhythmic breathing and the occasional scratch, shuffle or flutter of wings from the rafters overhead. Some pigeons must have found themselves sealed up in here. Kinda funny sounding pigeons.

"You hear that, Roy?" he said.

Dwayne called out from somewhere down below, "Ya know, Roy? I don't see nothin' special in this here barn."

"It's 'cause it's dark, that's why," said Roy in a half-shout, half-whisper.

The scratching and fluttering seemed to be growing louder, and Woodrow decided it couldn't be pigeons. At the least, pigeons would be cooing. Damn things wouldn't stop with the cooing. And there was none of that. So what could— bats! Were there bats up here? Woodrow shivered. "Roy?" he whispered.

"I'm just sayin', ya know," said Dwayne, "it seems like something' important in here, it'd be obvious. An' all I can see is the regular stuff."

Roy responded in the same shouted whisper, "There's somethin' and it's in here. Proof o' that is what happened to Darryl—"

"Damn shame about ol' Darryl," said Owen.

"—and all them soldier boys outside. They want it, we got it, and we can sort out the details later. Now you boys shut yer yaps and watch them doors." Roy thumped the floor of the loft, sending up a puff of dust and setting him off on a sneezing fit.

Roy stopped sneezing, and the scratching and fluttering that had been worrying Woodrow ceased. In the silence, listening only to his own breathing, feeling his heart rate slowing, Woodrow began to relax. And then something clapped him on the back.

Woodrow shuddered, and his heart hammered back to life, but somehow he managed not to jump three feet in the air or scream like a little girl. Damn that Roy, pranking him at a time like this. "Geez, Roy. Ya scared the hell outta me. I thought you was over there."

Roy didn't guffaw. He didn't slap Woodrow on the shoulder. He didn't congratulate him on his nerves of steel.

From halfway across the hayloft, Roy said, "Eh, Woodrow? Over where, now?"

"Then who—" Woodrow peered over his shoulder and into the compound eyes of a wasp as big as a housecat.

Chapter 38

SATURDAY

Wasp-self crushed the usurper in her mandibles, drove her stinger through the flimsy armor on its belly.

Pain, so intense it overwhelmed her other senses, rippled up through her abdomen. What in the *quivering of her thorax hairs* was the meaning of this?! Had the clumsy non-wasp stung her as she killed it? This would not stand. She would sting everything in the world for this! Starting with that gleaming thing hurtling toward her.

The tangled wreckage of his plane and the mutant wasp tumbled away from Hubert, shrinking ever smaller as they flipped past. The rush of wind made the radio squawking in his ears unintelligible.

Lightning Two dropped into view and everything froze in tableau.

A flare beneath the F-35's wing suddenly streaked away and disappeared in a flash as it reached the remains of Hubert's plane.

Pop.

Hubert blinked away the afterimage and stared at the spiky ball of black smoke that floated in the space where his jet had been. Then the scene oscillated gently back as Hubert pendulumed beneath a huge parachute.

"Someone's going to need to take Captain Pugslington for walkies," he said.

Beretta, leaning back against her car with her arms crossed, cast one last glance over her captives. The two militiamen—as they called themselves—that Yonda had retrieved sat in the shade, bound hand and foot, with simmering hatred in their eyes. Beside them, "ol' Jimmy" snored peacefully.

"Alright," she said. "So we have an understanding, then, Zach?" She pushed herself off the vehicle and turned her attention back to Zach.

He was actually shaking in his boots, his eyes zipping from one imposing member of her team to the next. "But, but, what if they shoot me?" he whined.

"Zach, honey," she said, "these are your brothers-in-arms. Your family. They're not going to shoot you." She grinned. "Bhalsim and Luile, here. *They* want to shoot you. But so long as you're being helpful..." She shrugged.

"I mean, by accident. Y'know. On account of bein' surprised an' all."

"Don't you worry. Just do as I say, and nobody will be surprised."

Zach looked at the ground, but finally nodded.

Beretta gently guided Zach in the direction of the barn. She imagined she could actually hear his boots squelching—the kid had been well hydrated. By the time they were a stone's throw away from the door, her boys had already taken up position, tasers at the ready.

Beretta nudged Zach.

He hesitated, lips trembling. He looked at her, then back at the barn, and just above a whisper, said, "Hey, fellahs." He cleared his throat and tried again, this time actually loud enough to be heard. "Hey, fellahs!"

Some indistinct shouting came back from the barn.

Zach continued, "Fellahs, we did it! Roy! We did it!"

A surly voice cut through the unintelligible grumbling coming from the barn. "Who's that? Who's out there?"

"It's me! It's Zach. Fellahs, we done it. We got 'em."

The barn responded, "Zach? He says it's Zach. Sounds like Zach. Zach, what you talkin' about?"

Beretta whispered in Zach's ear.

Zach shouted back, a little quaver in his voice, "ol' Jimmy said we could take 'em, an' he was right. We got 'em. We got 'em all. Come see."

"He says they got all the soldiers," barked the barn. "Yeah, that's what he says, Roy." A voice echoed faintly behind the door. "Roy wants to know how the hell you did that."

This. This was the kind of fun she really missed, cooped up with all that damned paperwork. It almost made a person hope for a national crisis. She was such a combat nerd! She suppressed a giggle and whispered in Zach's ear again.

Zach's eyes bulged, but he licked his lips and continued, "That woman what was with 'em, she was the leader. What's a woman know about military tactics, am I right?"

Some gruff laughter rumbled behind the door.

"An' we even caught one of 'em," said Zach, wringing his hands, "one of them soldiers, we caught 'im with his pants down. No foolin'."

The laughter erupted again, and the same angry voice said, "Oh, this I gotta see."

Beretta heard the bolt on the barn door slide back. She stepped away from Zach so she wasn't in direct line-of-sight with the door, and listened as it started to roll open with a hollow booming.

Colonel Pritchard climbed into his chair in the cockpit and shifted his butt until he was comfortably settled. He jacked his headset back into the console, then repositioned the cans on his ears. The springy black cord that tethered him to the radio bobbed and jiggled wildly against his shoulder.

"Agent Franks and Agent Reynolds are headed into the forward hold," he said. He glanced out the windshield, but they were still high enough that there was little to see but an expanse of blue sky above and hazy, splotchy colors below.

"Understood," said his copilot, Lieutenant Colonel Tucker. "I've kept us at the same rate of descent. It looks like we should be," he leaned forward to see something on the screen in front of him, "six minutes out of Albuquerque." He sat back and returned his focus to the iPad on his lap, poking and prodding the device like it owed him money.

"I hope you haven't been playing Pong on that thing the whole time I was out."

Tucker chuckled. "These emergency landings sure make a lot of extra paperwork."

"You're telling me."

"I was trying to get a leg up before things got busy." Tucker looked over at Pritchard. "You done many of these?"

Pritchard laughed. "Tons. But that was ages back."

"Yeah, it's been a while for me, too." Tucker laced his fingers together and flexed them this way and that. "Listen, Jon, you think the agents are going to get the gear down?"

"I hope so, Roge," said Pritchard. He gave Tucker a determined look. "But it's not like it's our first time around the block. If we can't lower the gear, we've still got plenty of fuel to—" Something dropped down in the periphery of his vision, and he turned to see what it was.

A small wasp writhed angrily on the instrumentation until it righted its body. It fluttered its wings and turned to face him.

"There's somethin' over here, Roy," said Woodrow, his voice trembling despite his hushed whisper. In the near darkness, Woodrow could hardly see the... *thing* staring back at him. But huge, shiny eyes and sudden twitching motions told him that This Was Very Bad.

"Shut it, wouldja," said Roy. "I'm tryin' to hear what the hell Zach's sayin' to Dwayne."

Woodrow held very still, and found himself reluctant to move even his lips. "It's on my shoulder, Roy!" he hissed. "I think— I think it's a alien."

"Goddammit, Woodrow, shut your yap. Dwayne's openin' the door an' I gotta see what the hell's goin' on." Roy huffed and mumbled, "Spoutin' nonsense at a time like this. Them movies puttin' crazy ideas in your head. Rottin' your brains. We gots what they all wants and you talkin' 'bout aliens!"

An icy clarity crept over Woodrow as the terror and adrenaline froze the moment in his mind. He had never actually liked Roy. And come to think of it, Roy had only ever treated Woodrow like he was someone to be tolerated. Why the hell had he ever tried so hard to please Roy? And how many other people had to look an alien in the face to realize their best friend was a son-of-a-bitch?

Sunlight lanced into the building as Dwayne hauled the sliding door open, illuminating the beast perched on Woodrow's shoulder. Its antennae quivered and its huge mandibles chattered sickeningly in Woodrow's ear.

He opened his mouth in a silent scream, his every muscle knotted, while his mind played through every one of those space alien movies that Roy had said were stupid. That insectoid face, those horrible jaws and sharp edges, the glistening exoskeleton—that's what they called it, yessir—this was not the friendly alien come to share its technology with mankind. These aliens were the scary aliens, come to lay waste to the Earth, to tear humans limb from limb with horrible wet crunches and blood spattering everywhere after first sneaking past the camera in shadow for a while so everything gets really really tense. And that's what happened to ol' Darryl, and Woodrow'd be the next, because here he'd been hiding in a darkened barn and the monster had snuck up on him and he'd been surprised and what good was he to the story anymore because he'd already done his part to make the angry crowd scene go off without a hitch.

The scream finally exploded from his lungs, accompanied by the full bodied spasming and scrambling that comes with the desperate desire not to be a pile of gore beneath a giant alien bug. As he flopped and twisted and kicked, the monster floated casually up into the air, grinding its bonecrushing mandibles, and staring down at him.

"Shoot it! Shoot it!" he screamed, pushing and sliding further and further out of the recesses of the hayloft. "Holy fucking jeezus—" And then Woodrow, too, sailed into the air.

Agents Franks and Reynolds unfolded the composite of torn magazine pages slowly and carefully. With every crinkle of the paper, Desmond had to resist the urge to cringe. He didn't want to move too quickly and risk stirring up the nest. It seemed like Reynolds was happy to follow his lead.

At last, they had it fully opened.

Desmond had made sure they tiled the sheet large enough to completely wall off the front of the hold, anticipating that they probably wouldn't be able to separate themselves from the wasps any other way. But the practical reality was awkward as hell. The thing was so big that they had to let it curl over their heads in order to avoid stepping on it. And, naturally, that totally obscured their view.

Maybe that was a blessing. He'd already seen enough of that churning mound to turn his stomach. Staring at it as he approached probably wouldn't help his nerves any.

"Rush in on three?" hissed Reynolds.

Shit. If he were a tiny, winged vessel of rage, what would be more likely to set him off? A huge thing rushing up to his home, or a huge thing sidling up nice and slow? He'd probably be pissed either way. So which would be more likely to get Desmond and Reynolds killed? Shit. He shook his head. "Let's ease up real slow."

They stepped forward at a glacial pace.

With only a view of the carpet beneath his feet, Desmond found himself concentrating on the sounds in the room. The constant hiss of the air conditioning and drone of the plane engines—so ubiquitous that he'd stopped hearing it hours ago—had completely masked the noise of the wasps. He noticed it now, though. The buzzing and humming of dozens, perhaps hundreds, of tiny wings. The scritch and scratch of whatever the hell it was that wasps did on their nests. Seriously, though. What were they doing? Making it bigger, maybe? They couldn't just be milling around because they were bored. Could a wasp get bored? If they could get bored, that would probably mean they had fun, too. What would a wasp do for fun? Get a drink with his boys after a hard day of scritching and scratching? Hey fellahs, I know this flower where the nectar's cheap and the girls are fast and easy! Yeah, not likely. And, Jesus, were they getting more agitated or was his imagination getting the best of him?

He glanced at Reynolds. Despite the cool air in the plane, sweat was dripping off his nose.

Just how much longer—there! The nose gear controls! He locked eyes with his partner and they stopped. He bobbed his head steadily in a three count, and then they slapped the sheet up to the ceiling.

In a desperate rush of activity—the tape shipping and shooping as they peeled it from their clothing—they slapped tape onto the pages and ceiling. Franks focused on getting the barrier hung, figuring he'd go back to close any small gaps after the bigger job was done. He hoped to God that a swarm of angry wasps would be too distracted by the arrival of an entire wall to immediately track down the few little spaces they could slip through. He dropped down to the floor, pasting the sheet to the carpet as fast as he could.

Smack!

Franks snapped his head to the side as Reynolds whopped the wall with his primary weapon twice more.

"I have had it with these motherfucking wasps on this motherfucking plane!" said Reynolds.

Franks was nonplused and almost stopped taping. "Really, Reynolds?"

"Look," Reynolds smacked another wasp before sealing a gap, "you know someone had to say it."

Franks shook his head. He dropped his magazine and yanked opened the panel to reveal the manual nose gear release—a crank folded into a cubby hole. He lifted it up and locked it into place. "I'm lowering the gear."

"Better—" Whack! "—make it—" Whop! "—snappy." Pap!

Franks spun the crank easily a half-dozen revolutions before resistance practically stopped him dead. He braced himself and heaved against the crank, starting a slow but steady turn. He must be fighting against the wind resistance now. With both hands white-knuckled on the metal rod, he made rotating the crank a whole body endeavor.

The paper wall by his head rustled and pocked.

Chapter 39

SATURDAY

"Oh—" said Pritchard, looking at the wasp that had just appeared in front of him. He glanced up to where it had presumably dropped from.

Wasps burbled out of a vent in the ceiling.

"—shit!"

Tucker's hand shot out and twisted the vent closed in a flash, stopping the flow of wasps and crushing several that hadn't made it all the way through. He gasped and slapped his hand down on the instrument panel, leaving behind a smear of insect carnage.

"Jesus, Roge!"

"Kill the rest of 'em," said Tucker.

Pritchard was climbing out of his seat before he realized what he was doing. He only narrowly managed not to tumble to the floor as the taut cord pulled the headset from his ears. Had they stung Tucker? Kill them with what? How could he land with wasps on the controls? He heard the high-pitched whine of tiny wings.

Tucker was trying to scramble out of his own seat, but he was belted in. His breathing was ragged as he struggled with the clasp.

They were minutes away from landing and Pritchard had to get back to the controls. But if he got stung, too— "There's nothing here," he blurted. "There's nothing to smash them with."

"The logbook. Hit 'em with the logbook."

Pritchard heard the zing of a bug nearby and dodged away. His eyes danced, trying to track each of the buzzing threats lazily arcing around the cabin. "It's all digital now. There's no book."

Tucker twisted in his seat, and with a scritching rip, tore the tablet free from the velcro straps on his leg. "For Chrissakes, Jon, hit 'em with the freaking iPad," he wheezed, waving it behind the chair.

Pritchard snatched up the tablet. The screen lit up with brightly colored icons. "What app do I use?" Jesus, what the hell was he saying?! He squeezed the thing tightly with both hands and went in swinging.

Beretta heard the door stop and then the barn's spokesvoice said, "Alright, Zach, where's them soldier boys? Say, what the hell happened to your pants—"

Someone screeched deeper in the barn, and Beretta instinctually coiled her muscles for the sprint toward the barn door. During the ages long process of launching her body forward, the scenario about to play out in the barn flashed through her mind. This wasn't a simple soldiers-versus-militiamen anymore. Now it was soldiers-versus-militiamen-and-*fucking-mutant-wasps*.

Her ploy with Zach had opened the door, but her team had to get inside before the inevitable shitstorm erupted in there. "Go!" she shouted as she took that first step forward.

Fortunately, she could see that her team had anticipated her order.

Inside of a heartbeat, the big man framed in the doorway, distracted by the shouting within, took Bhalsim's taser in the back. Click-click-click and he sank to his knees.

Bhalsim dropped the taser and grabbed the man, who flopped like a ragdoll while Bhalsim heaved him clear of the entry.

Luile and Yonda swept through the door an instant later, the bottleneck giving Beretta the extra second she needed to catch up to them. She planted a hand on Yonda's back as they pushed into the barn so he'd know where she was, and the satchel containing Plan B jostled against her body.

Luile veered off along the front wall of the barn toward a shocked-looking farmer with a rifle. The man didn't get the chance to lift his weapon before the two taser darts struck him and wiped the surprise off his face.

"Shoot it!" someone screamed from up in the hayloft.

Beretta scanned the familiar room for the two other men who were supposed to be in here. Great. Guess they're both up in the loft. She urged Yonda forward with steady pressure on his back. Deploying Plan B was her priority. She'd extract these damned fools from the hayloft after that. If possible.

The flailing arms of a lanky man appeared at the edge of the loft. "Shoot it!" he screamed again, before propelling himself blindly into the open air. His limbs scissored and jerked wildly before gravity wrapped her hand around him and yanked him to the floor. His body landed with a meaty thud-crack, his head bouncing off the concrete floor. And then he was still.

She and Yonda reached the pile of knees and elbows in a few more strides, and Beretta stopped them with a quick tug of her hand. Yonda's head was tilted toward the loft. He must be thinking the same thing she was. Anyway, this spot would do well enough for Plan B.

The meatsack beside her sucked in a startled breath as she slammed down her satchel. "Ow?" it said.

Not dead, huh? Well, no time to waste. "Yonda, extract this one. Go!"

Yonda turned and tossed the dazed militiaman over his shoulder without hesitation or apparent effort while Beretta peeled the bag off of her bomb.

"What the shit is going on?!" bellowed a voice from the hayloft.

Beretta watched the loft while her fingers danced across her vest. Her hand closed over the sharp edges of the detonator clipped to her and she toggled it on.

A round face appeared over the ledge above her, ruddy with effort and fury. It was joined quickly by the business end of a pistol, spitting fire and lead as its owner punched it toward Beretta.

Metal twanged and thunked around her as bullets widely missed their marks. She looked back down at the ordinance on the floor while blindly dumping a few rounds from her M9 in the direction of her new friend. She flicked a switch and a red light winked at her. She popped off a couple more shots and sighed. The light turned orange and her bomb beeped. Awesome.

She turned back toward the hayloft. The combatant peeked over the side again, and she brushed him back, splintering the boards around him with several slugs from her sidearm. Movement in the rafters caught her eye. Shitballs. Time was definitely up.

"Last chance to walk out of here," shoutcd Beretta, her voice surprisingly loud in the stark silence between pistol shots. "Throw down your weapons."

The pistol reappeared over the lip of the hayloft, firing wildly. "You can't tread on me, Government! I know my rights!"

Not likely. But screw this guy. He had his chance. She returned fire while sprinting toward the door, and then she was clear in the dazzling sunshine.

Bhalsim slammed the door home behind her. She squinted against the bright light, seeking her bearings amongst the adrenaline-fueled sensory overload. All but Bhalsim were ahead of her, hauling the militiamen away from the barn. Hardly a minute had passed since they breached the door. She shook her head. "Everyone get clear of the barn and take cover," she said.

Desmond's vision tunnelled and he tuned out the sounds of the room, instead hearing only the muffled rush of blood in his ears. There was nothing but the metal crank, slick with the sweat from his palms, and the hammering of his heart. He settled into a rhythm, like he was in the gym on a rowing machine, heaving his entire body back and forth with each revolution. Unbidden, but welcome, a 'one, two' count pushed all of the other thoughts from his mind. He was one with the crank. Nothing mattered but the rippling of the weak yellow lights on the shiny surface. Turning the crank was breathing. Turning the crank was life. Turning the crank was—

Reynolds yelped and cursed.

The buzzing of the insects and the drone of the engines, the flexing and straining of the paper barrier, the ripe smell of his own sweat, all crashed in on Desmond.

"They got me, partner" said Reynolds. "You'd better hurry this up."

Desmond looked at Reynolds, shaking off the daze.

With his back turned, the other agent crushed another assailant with the glossy roll of his limited-edition Italian Vogue magazine. He clutched a shorter weapon in his off-hand—a Readers' Digest? *That* couldn't have come from the girls—and sucked in a ragged breath. He dropped to one knee.

The crank turned halfway through another rotation, went kerchunk, and seized. Desmond tugged with everything he had left, but it wouldn't budge. That's it, then. Hopefully the gear was down, because there wasn't anything more he could do. "It's done," he said. "Time to evac."

Desmond crawled the few feet to his partner, and then guided Reynolds's arm over his shoulder. He stood, lifting Reynolds to his feet, but his partner was already desperately gasping for breath. There was no way he'd manage to climb up that ladder on his own, and between the narrow hatch and his recent full body workout, Desmond couldn't carry him out either. With his free hand, he patted wildly at his pockets. Where the hell had he put it? Ah! He snatched out the EpiPen, popped the cap with his thumb and jabbed it into Reynolds's thigh.

Was he imagining tiny legs poking through the seams of the makeshift wall? He hoped to God that the medicine was enough, because their time was up.

Desmond directed his partner down the narrow passage, lifting and sidestepping to the best of his ability, all the while watching for pursuers. He could hear Reynold's breathing improving a little with each new lungful. They stopped. The ladder, thank God. "Climb," he said. "Climb!"

Reynolds hugged the rungs like a boxer after ten punishing rounds. He clumsily searched for a step, finally making purchase, and then lifting himself a few inches.

Desmond grabbed at the other agent and pushed him up the ladder, urging him to go faster. He couldn't possibly hear the paper tearing. That was just his imagination getting carried away. But couldn't Reynolds climb any faster.

A lone wasp, a little bigger than the others he'd seen so far, bumbled casually down the passageway. It pinged off the wall, then the bundle of luggage, but the inevitability of its course was certain.

Reynolds was almost out, but Desmond wouldn't be able to escape before the wasp—Jesus, he'd left his weapon behind. As the wasp closed on him, he raised his hands and adjusted his stance. Mr. Miyagi, eat your heart out. Real men don't use their karate on house flies. In a blur, he neutralized the bug with his bare knuckles. He pulled his fist back from the wall, leaving the twitching carcass glued with its own splattered guts.

The light changed, and he looked up. Reynolds was clear. He heaved himself up the ladder, scrambling out the hatch.

Reynolds slammed the panel closed and they both collapsed.

Roy clenched his eyes shut and hugged his free arm around his head. He yanked his gun hand back from the edge as that soldier-bitch's shots threw dust and splinters at him. And then, with a rolling boom, the light in the barn winked out.

He listened for a second, but there was nothing down below. Did he run them off? Very slowly, he uncurled his body. He clenched his teeth, his heart hammering up into his throat. Ah, fuck it! He popped his head up.

Nothin' and nobody. Just dust dancing in the few shafts of light below.

Hells yeah! He'd done it. Just him, not any of them other fellahs. He knew they didn't have what it took, anyway. "That's right! Run!" he shouted.

He shuffled and scrambled, stopped himself before he tumbled head first over the edge, and then got himself turned around. That's right. *He* did it. *Roy*. He'd been carrying all them boys on his back for so long, and this just proved it. He scrape-thumped his way down the ladder, his hands trembling each time he shifted his grip, the butt of his pistol whacking into every rung. His boot squished when he reached the floor. What the hell did he spill down his pant leg?

He spun around, waving his pistol at nothing in particular. "You want it and I've got it," he shouted. "No government's gonna step on my rights. And you keep runnin', 'cause nothin's gonna move me from—"

A little orange light on the floor caught his eye. Roy didn't remember that being there before.

Somewhere above him, something went,"brrrzzzzpt." A weight landed on his shoulder and his shirt twisted all funny. The little voice in his head that Roy regarded as Rational Thought got very very quiet. He looked at his shoulder and something with very large eyes and antennas looked back at him.

He blinked.

The thing at his feet went, "beep."

He looked down and the orange light turned green. "Eh?" he said.

For an instant, the flash of light actually threw a shadow in front of Beretta, despite the bright sunshine. Heat rippled over her head and shoulders. *Wha-boom!* thundered in her ears. Even with distance and an SUV between herself and the explosion, she still felt like someone kicked her in the back. Her ears popped, and sound and a high-pitched ringing started to filter in again. She looked down at her fist, clenched tightly over the detonator, and she lifted her thumb off the button. She sighed. She did not like Plan B.

With the pitter, patter, thump and bump of kindling that used to be barn raining down behind her, she glanced over at her boys and their prisoners. Everyone looked alert and no one was screaming, so that was good. She stood and looked through the tinted windows of the Escalade at what remained of the barn.

With a creaking, crackling groan, one of the few standing pieces of the structure collapsed into the heap of smoldering debris that had been sucked back into the center of the space after the initial fireball. Only a few small fires still burned, and there wasn't any danger of them spreading.

They'd check it, of course, but nothing that had been in there during the explosion could have survived. She rested her hands on the grips of her holstered pistols and shook her head. That was it. At least, the fun part, anyway. Next up, paperwork. For her sins.

Pritchard had never felt like this in the cockpit of a plane. He'd test piloted experimental jets, flown nighttime bombing runs over enemy territory, landed on that postage stamp they call a carrier. But he'd never felt mind numbing terror inside of a plane. It had always been like an extension of his body. Sure, there'd been anxiety about the danger of a mission. But he'd been in total control of the aircraft. He'd always been completely certain that the plane would do precisely what he wanted, whenever he wanted.

He brought the iPad down in a two-fisted overhead swing, crushing another of the creatures with a pop. The glass spiderwebbed and a sad computer face appeared just before the screen winked out.

He'd never felt trapped on a plane. And he'd certainly never felt his mind just go blank. Not like now.

He searched the air for more wasps and his glance took in the view out the windshield. My God, they were getting close to the ground! Somebody had better pull up— He looked at his copilot.

Tucker was feebly tugging at his restraints with a hand that had blown up like a balloon. He sounded like he was trying to suck the last drop of a soda out of an empty cup.

Jesus Christ, no one was flying the plane!

Pritchard dropped the tablet and hurdled over his chair. He grabbed the yolk and leveled out of their descent while scanning the the instruments. The nose gear light was lit, thank God for small mercies. The agents had done it.

Bzzt. Clap. He felt the gooey remains of a bug against the back of his neck and then he felt a burning pain radiate away from the spot. Fuuuuuuck!

How much time before he couldn't fly? His hands danced across the controls like a concert pianist. He lit the 'fasten seatbelt' indicator and lowered the rear landing gear. As the pain burned hotter, he eased the plane into the final approach.

What the hell happened to his headset, anyway? He pulled it up by its cord and flopped the cups over his ears.

"—ease respond, Air Force One," said a casual, lazy voice in his ear.

Pritchard pushed-to-talk and said, "Mayday, mayday." His voice was as disinterested as ever, but unusually raspy. "We're on final approach, Control. My copilot is incapacitated and I'm injured. Our nose gear may be compromised."

The tightness in Pritchard's chest was increasing and Barry White started singing a lullaby in his ear. Damn, that was kind of strange. But outside the window, the runway loomed up dead center. Good runway. Stay!

His chair kicked him hard in the ass. Crap. A landing fit for a carrier. Someone would give him crap for that. If he lived. He reversed the thrust on the engines and stepped on the brakes.

White sprites washed over his vision. Screw 'em. Colonel Jon Pritchard would show 'em how it was done. He held the nose up in the air for a couple of centuries until it finally eased down and kissed the tarmac. Textbook.

He smiled and went off to dance with Barry White.

Chapter 40

SATURDAY

Court kept both hands clenched tightly around the side rail of the stretcher as she walked beside it. Her nerves were absolutely fried at this point, and the organized chaos around her was pushing her to the brink of losing it altogether. She could feel her shoulders shaking, and if she weren't hanging onto a metal bar with all her might, her hands would be outright trembling.

When the plane had hit the runway, she'd peed a little. She just knew it. Thank god for her black clothes. She'd have absolutely died of embarrassment if anyone had been able to tell. At least she didn't vomit. She almost did. Britney did.

And then the plane stopped, and the flight crew opened the doors, and the girls were trying to get off, and an army of paramedics and men in white moonsuits were flooding on, and the whole thing was chaos and gridlock, and she *did* live tweet that, because she just had to do something with her thumbs.

Moonsuits! Seriously, what the hell?! It was like something out of a movie about a nuclear melt-down— her stomach flopped over. Jesus, could it be? Was she feeling nauseated because there was actually a radiation leak on the plane and ohmygod did she really just think that thought, because there was no nuclear reactor on an airplane.

"So, where's the beach, anyway?" said Harmony.

That yanked Court back into the here and now, with all the flashing emergency lights, and ambulance and firetruck sirens. They'd made it a couple hundred yards from the plane, the group of girls forming an honor guard around Celeste on the stretcher. She looked past Jessica, standing on the opposite side, to Harmony's vacant expression. How *had* that girl made it into college?

"We're in Albuquerque," said Jessica.

"What part of California is that?" said Harmony.

"Miss Goodson." A stern looking man, his face framed by the ridiculous, poofy white hood of his coveralls, jogged up to the group. He held out a phone. "Miss Goodson, I have the president on the line for you."

Jessica accepted the phone and the man turned to leave.

He nearly collided with Desmond, who was just catching up to the group. Desmond looked exhausted.

"Hello?" said Jessica. She plugged her other ear with her finger. "Daddy? What? Hang on a sec, I can't hear you." She pulled the phone away from her ear and fumbled with it for a moment.

"—you okay? Jessica?" The president's voice was squeaky and tinny from the little speaker, but immediately recognizable to Court from televised speeches.

"Daddy, we're fine. We're all out of the airplane."

"Oh, thank God."

Like, really, the president. Like, really really. Not that Court cared, or anything. He's just Jessica's dad, so, not really a surprise. So, yeah, the president of the United States is on a speakerphone two feet away. Whatever. Court eased her death-grip on the rail by a couple of foot-pounds.

"The airport looks like some kind of chemical emergency site," Jessica looked back over her shoulder at Air Force One, "with all kinds of people in hazmat coveralls and masks. What the hell is going on?"

That was a fair question, right? Court leaned in just a little closer.

"You scared me half to death," continued President Goodson. "Don't ever scare me like that again—"

Jessica rolled her eyes.

Celeste fidgeted on the stretcher, twisting and turning to see what there was to see. She spotted Desmond and laid back down on the gurney with one hand placed theatrically on her forehead.

"—going to bring you back home right this instant," said the president.

"Daddy, what about California?"

"Desmond?" said Celeste weakly. "Desmond, are you here?"

"And no more airplanes," chirped the phone. "We'll put you on a bus—is there anything I should worry about with a bus, Doctor?"

Desmond shuffled amongst the girls until he was walking beside Celeste. "Yeah, I'm here."

"—what do you mean armadillo research? What the hell are armadillo good for anyway—no, never mind. A boat. We'll put you on a boat."

Jessica pinched the bridge of her nose. "Daddy, I don't think there's a water route from New Mexico to DC."

Celeste waved Desmond in a little closer, and he leaned forward.

"No, a boat's a bad idea. Probably mutant sharks with laser eyes or something."

Jessica met Court's gaze, pointed at the phone and mouthed, 'what the hell?' "Daddy! We're going to California."

Celeste grabbed Desmond's lapels in vice-grips and pulled his lips to hers. His eyes bulged, but apparently she'd overpowered him.

"No, you're coming home—"

"Daddy, we're finishing the trip. I'll have Desmond—" Jessica looked at the spectacle and chuckled. "I'll get something settled and let you know."

Court strained to hear what the President was saying, but missed it.

Jessica just nodded her head and rolled her eyes. "Listen, Daddy, have you told Mom about this?"

"Oh. My. God. Your. Mother. Will. Kill. Me."

"Ok, Daddy, well you go talk to Mom, and I'll let you know when we get to California." She hung up the phone before the president could say anything else.

Court's mouth dropped open a little. "Did you just hang up on the president of the United States?"

Jessica smiled. "Negotiation tactic."

"Mmmmm," said Celeste, finally allowing a few inches of space to appear between herself and Desmond.

"But— but he's *the president*," said Court.

"Yeah, well." Jessica looked at the phone in her hand, then glanced around behind her at the anonymous crew of rescue workers. She shrugged. "We take our arguing pretty seriously in my family."

Celeste cocked her head to the side and made pouty lips at Desmond's dumbfounded expression. "Well, subtle wasn't working on you!"

"*Subtle!*" Jessica leaned back and laughed heartily. "Come on," she said, wiping tears away from her eyes, "let's go see about that beach for Harmony."

Epilogue

NEXT WEEK

Reid Ransom lounged at the restaurant table with an air of proprietorship. He'd have done that anyway, but in this particular case he did actually own it—an acquisition he'd made last fall on a whim, for a staggeringly huge sum of money. Not the most expensive meal he'd ever eaten, but close. And a mere six months later, he was already turning a profit.

His waitress leaned over the table to refill his water glass and Reid smiled. He smiled at the delightful view of the terrace garden, at the obscene profits this venture was turning, at the bombshell of the blond variety, clad in a dress cut down to her naval and slit up to her waist—with the sort of cleavage that inspired poetry and the kind of legs that caused car wrecks—currently pouring water into his glass. The light glinting off his pearly whites illuminated the depths of those tantalizing valleys. Perhaps, after this lunch meeting concluded, he should have a private word with her about her career goals.

Yes, the man he'd put in charge of this place had struck precisely the balance he'd wanted. The staff was beautiful enough to ensure that the fat cat patrons got a hard-on, their attire just understated enough not to outshine any mistresses in attendance, and the restaurant as a whole expensive and exclusive enough to keep the wives from objecting.

As he watched his server's perfect ass sashay away, he brought his attention back to the phone pressed to his ear. What Tarantino-esque moniker had they chosen this time? Oh, that's right.

"You know, Mr. Black," he said, "I hadn't seen that in the news. You would think anyone who refueled planes for a living would know better than to smoke on the job. It's just terrible that accidents like that can happen."

A serious man in a black suit stepped into the otherwise empty dining room, looked around and then mumbled something into his sleeve.

"Well, it looks like my lunch date has arrived, Mr. Black. I'm going to have to check in with you later." He hung up and pocketed the phone as he stood to welcome his guest.

His waitress, all radiant smiles and tanned skin, lead the way, with his guest tugged along by the mesmerizing sway of her...*hips*. Reid beamed at his little joke. Yes, he'd definitely clear his schedule for some alone time with this girl. "Bill!" he said. "Welcome, welcome!"

Vice President William Rose finally looked up, without a hint of embarrassment. "Reid," he said, "it's so good to see you."

They shook hands and Reid gestured for them to sit.

Their server departed and the vice president shamelessly watched her go.

Reid felt a twinge of animal jealousy but squelched the urge to lash out.

"Well, Reid," said Bill, once the girl was out of sight, "it's such a pity that our little project didn't work out."

"Easy come, easy go." Reid shrugged. "Nothing ventured, nothing gained, and all that."

"I'm prepared to accept your expertise in the matter." The vice president squinted into the glare from Reid's grin.

"And don't worry, Bill. There'll be plenty more opportunities to turn a profit."

"Alex."

Alex Chumley—just Chumley to, well, pretty much everybody—massaged his temples gently and took slow deep breaths.

"Alex?"

His head throbbed with a whomp-whomp-whomp that he was pretty sure was not actually audible to anyone else. But, then, everyone seemed to be raising their voices at him—which was not helping with the throbbing, thank you—so maybe the sound was bothering everybody.

"Chumley!"

Chumley winced and opened his eyes. Then he winced again. The fluorescent lights in this lab must be brighter than the usual spec. There was a reason that they recommended certain bulbs for use in work environments. There were probably studies. There must be. He'd look that up. Inconsiderate to choose unreasonably bright lights and make the people who work here suffer—

"Chumley, are you feeling all right?"

He squinted up at his new boss, Doctor Vanessa Schneider. She was all worry and concern. That was kind of a nice change. His old boss, Doctor Zmeyansky, was all disgust and disdain. He was actually the reason that Chumley found himself across the country, in some godforsaken desert, experimenting with...*armadillos.* That's how Zmeyansky had said it. Dripping with venom. And kind of smug. The bastard.

He glanced at Doctor Schneider's patiently waiting face. Oh, right. "It's nothing, Doctor. Just a little headache." He attempted a smile.

"Ok." She nodded. "Don't push yourself too hard. And no need to be so formal. Call me Vanessa." She smiled and squeezed his shoulder.

"Thanks, uh, Vanessa. But I'll be fine. Really."

She squeezed his shoulder again and continued on her way.

Chumley took a deep breath and looked at the lab table in front of him. What was it he was supposed to be doing? Oh, yeah. Mixing these samples. He picked up the pipette. Add exactly zero-point-seven-five-cc of the active to sample A. And then exactly zero-point-seven-five-cc of the active to sample B. God, the monotony of it all. So worth the mountain of debt he'd racked up earning that degree.

He probably should have just quit, rather than uprooting his whole life and coming all the way out to New Mexico. But in this economy...

Exactly zero-point-seven-five-cc—

And when he'd told Alison, his girlfriend, she'd hardly even seemed upset. Which was kind of telling, now that he thought about it. Because he'd only been gone, what, like two days, when she'd called and said that the whole long distance relationship thing just wasn't working for her. That she missed him too much, and it was tearing her up, and really, she needed a clean break, for her own sanity. And she'd said all that to his damn voicemail. And when he'd called her back, some *guy* picked up her phone. WTF!

Whomp-whomp-whomp. Deep breath.

Exactly zero-point-seven-five-cc of the active to sample B.

Did he already do that one? Nah. Nah, he didn't think so. Whatever.

Anyway, that was last night. He was so upset, he'd drowned his sorrows. He'd made it through almost two whole beers before he passed out.

God, Chumley, you can't even do that right, you freaking lightweight.

Note from the Author

Thanks for reading *operation: BLACKFLAG.* Seriously. I'm psyched that you read my novel. I know that there are so many great books out there to read and not enough time to read them all. So I really appreciate the time you spent with my story. And I hope you enjoyed it.

Please consider leaving a rating or review on Amazon, Goodreads, or wherever you acquired this book. Reviews help other readers decide which books are worth their time. And hearing what readers thought of my novel is pretty cool, too.

For updates on what I'm working on, follow me on Google+ at +Richard Kendrick (https://plus.google.com/+RichardKendrick/). And if you'd like me to notify you when I release a new book, you can join my mail list here: http://eepurl.com/bwQFZ5. I'll even throw in a free short story, just for signing up.

Keep flipping these pages for a sample of my young adult steampunk adventure novel, *Phrases of Light*. And keep your eyes peeled for the riveting sequel to *operation: BLACKFLAG*, *Armadillo-nado**.

*As the fate of the world hangs in the balance, the perfect genetically modified armadillo meets the perfect storm. But will one armadillo be enough to save humanity?**

Yeah, actually, that might be a little too ridiculous, even for me.*

***But I wrote it anyway.

About the Author

Richard J. Kendrick proofreads deadly serious nonfiction by day and scribbles fantasy when he can find a moment. He spends the rest of his time spoiling his family and riding his bike.

operation: BLACKFLAG is his second novel.

An excerpt from

Phrases of Light

by
Richard J. Kendrick

In a land where written works are held for ransom and current events are shared in song, three prodigious teens chase rumors of fantastical devices and discover a secret which could change the world.

From the back cover:

John was so out of his depth. No matter how prodigious his talent, the Multi Guild never trained him how to go on a date. So John just blurted it out, to impress a cute girl, to end an awkward silence: A boilerless steam engine. Just a ridiculous rumor from some unknown minstrel. Not even a mention in the Archive, where the Multis meticulously catalogued all of the world's knowledge. But for Caprice, an aspiring young engineer, it was something new, a mystery, an invitation to adventure.

And John could hardly sit by and let her rush off to parts unknown all by herself, could he? Not when this spontaneous quest was all his fault and the notion of a second date was still undetermined.

Lucky for the pair that Lumin, a Speaker trained in an ancient martial art, is hanging around when they promptly stumble into trouble. But Lumin's got worries of his own, including occasionally hearing voices, and a secret that he's increasingly certain is tied up with Caprice's quest.

Chapter 1

Lumin retched onto the dirt below him, his weight supported tremulously on his hands and knees. Despite the searing pain where the great brick of compacted scrap had scraped across his mind as it fell past him, he was aware of the five pebbles beneath his hands: three smooth, one with a sharp edge, and another with a crack in it. He felt the presence of the towers of compacted and bundled scrap metal looming over him, the mound of trash yet to be sorted some yards away.

His shoulders burned where the girl's hands touched him and thunder rumbled above Lumin's head.

"Are you alright?" said the thunder.

Lumin opened his eyes and saw all too clearly what had once been his breakfast. Lights flashed before him like an after-image, but of nothing he'd looked at. He resisted the urge to close his eyes again.

He Spoke and the lights stopped flashing, his shoulders stopped burning, and the entire world stepped back from his body.

"Are you alright?" said the girl.

Lumin spat and then nodded slowly. He sat up and the girl took a step back.

"You?" he said.

"I'm fine."

He got to his feet, grimacing slightly against the throbbing pain in his mind, and began to brush dust off his pant legs. His body appeared to be uninjured.

"You're lucky I came by just then," he said. "This is hardly a safe place to be wandering around."

"Mr. Baldwin didn't mention I'd be here?" she said.

Lumin looked at her. Moments before, he'd seen the girl. But he hadn't looked at her. Thousands of pounds of falling metal, lazily arcing toward the girl, had seemed of more immediate concern. Moving both himself and her out of its path had taken all of his concentration.

Now he realized, despite her small size, she was not a child. Middle teens, he figured, perhaps even his own age. Her eyes met his squarely.

"He mentioned there'd be someone," said Lumin, "but you weren't what I'd expected." But this was true only because he hadn't considered what to expect. Everything about her appearance screamed purpose, from her washed-out blue cover-alls to the strange harness looping across her shoulders and chest and waist, from which dangled a small variety of tools. Lumin was the one who looked out of place, wearing the dark-gray silk uniform of his House, with its sash crisscrossing the breast of his tunic and tied at his waist.

His glance came back up to her face. She hadn't looked away from him. He felt himself start to blush and looked away from her to the wreckage that had nearly crushed him.

"Anyway, you should be more careful out here," said Lumin. "I've got a lot of ground to cover; I may not be nearby should there be trouble."

But even here in the wreckage he began to see purpose: cables and pulleys he hadn't noticed before.

"Thanks for watching out for me," she said.

A shadow of doubt began to creep over him. The voice of his teacher called from the back of his mind. Had he failed to observe? Despite all the praise, all his confidence, had he erred at such a basic level?

"You were in danger, weren't you?"

"Thanks for watching out for me," she said. She smiled.

The voice of his teacher called again, pushing closer to the surface of his thoughts— but this wasn't right, this voice wasn't right—

Lumin awoke. His mind felt as though it were swelling against his skull. He breathed out slowly and pushed the pain away from his consciousness, but not so far as to lose track of it.

He rolled up on his side and reached across the bed. His hand fell through the open air and he caught himself just before tumbling out.

"The hell?" he said. Was he on the wrong side? In the morning light, glowing orange through paper window blinds, the room seemed altogether too small. For that matter, the bed was too small. He sat up.

"Why am I here?" he said. Lumin climbed out of bed and stumbled down the hallway, his limbs sluggish with sleep, each footfall reminding him of the pain at the back of his mind. He heard running water and headed toward the kitchen.

The long and narrow kitchen glowed brightly in the morning sun. His mother stood at the sink, her long, dark brown hair haloed with light from the windows behind her. She looked up as he entered.

"Morning Mom," said Lumin. "Wow. You look great."

She smiled. "You're sweet," she said, and leaned out and kissed him on the cheek. She turned back to the sink.

"Hey, do you have any idea why I woke up in my old—" Lumin turned toward the sound of fork on plate coming from the table behind him. His father sat at the table, his gaze fixed on the greenery in the yard beyond the kitchen windows, a subtle look of contemplation on his face. He appeared to be an older version of Lumin, sharing his dimpled chin, dark hair, blue eyes, and the characteristic bump on his nose that was so typical of the House dla-W^{h}inza (though Lumin's bump was slightly softened by his mother's influence). He blindly shoveled some eggs into his mouth.

The pain began to rush forward, as if detecting a gap in Lumin's defenses.

"What's that, dear?" said his mother, not looking up from the sink.

"We've got to do something about this yard, today, Lumin," said his father. "And don't say you've got to study. You can take a few hours out for your old man." He looked down at his eggs and chuckled. "You wouldn't believe how jealous some of the other dads are. They can hardly get their kids to study, and I'll have to drag you away from it."

Lambent looked up at his son. "Oh, come on, it's just a little yard work." He laughed. "Who knew the secret to motivating youths was the threat of yard work? When the other parents learn of this, Candesce, all the children will devote themselves to study. Our House will rise to glory. They'll remember me in song—"

"This can't— it's not—" Lumin backed away.

"Help your father, Lumin," said Candesce. She looked up from the sink.

Lumin's shoulder clipped the archway between the kitchen and the hall and he stumbled. "This isn't right," he said.

"Lumin?" said Candesce. She knelt beside him where he had fallen and took his arm, her hands dripping. "Are you alright, sweetheart?"

"It's just a little yard work," said Lambent. He smiled nervously. He stepped forward but hesitated.

Lumin noticed his ragged breathing over the knot in his stomach. "I can't— this can't— I have to get out of here." He started to scramble down the hall, against his mother's grip, away from the kitchen.

"Sweetheart, you're not even dressed."

Lumin pulled against her grip.

"Stop," she said.

Lumin turned to her and their eyes met. She pulled him off the floor.

"Come with me," she said, and steered him back toward his bedroom, keeping her body between his and the kitchen.

Lambent stepped forward. "Son?" he said.

Candesce shot a glance over her shoulder and Lambent froze. She gently directed Lumin down the hall.

Lambent wilted onto his chair.

Chapter 2

John Sevaschen straightened his vest carefully on its hanger. The dozens of metal data cards covering the right front of the garment and surrounding the half-sleeve tinkled softly with each tug. He stared at it, unseeing. "I'm an idiot," he said.

His roommate, Nathan Thogmartin, sighed. "Yeah," he said. "Yeah, you are." He pulled off his other shoe and kicked the pair of them under the bed.

"All I had to do was make a little conversation. I mean, there was no rush, or anything. We were right there. But no!"

"Mmhmm." Thogmartin tossed what had earlier been his crisp, white, wing-tip shirt onto his bed, where it was shortly joined by his no longer sharply pressed black trousers, leaving him in his undershirt and shorts. He dropped to the floor and began doing push-ups.

John sat on his own bed across the room, looking toward the closet. "It just," he said. He looked down at the card reader strapped to his left thigh. "It caught me off guard." He began to unbuckle the reader. "I mean, I hardly ever talk to cute girls."

"That's true," said Thogmartin

"Shut up." John released the second buckle and lifted the reader off his leg. He paused. "Finally, there's this cute girl, and she seems smart and everything, and I just answer her question and she walks away. Just a little conversation, and maybe I'd have a date or something." John placed the card reader on its shelf in his closet, squaring it with the ledge.

Thogmartin let his breath out in a series of hisses timed to his push-ups. Freckles had blossomed all over his skin from the exercise. "You shouldn't dwell on it," he said. "That only leads to regret and masturbation." A rolled up pair of socks bounced off the back of his head.

"You shut up."

Thogmartin laughed and collapsed on the floor. He rolled onto his back.

John's gaze drifted back to the horizon. "Maybe she'll come back," said John.

"Yeah?"

John's eyes snapped back to Thogmartin, who began a series of crunches. "I mean," he said, "maybe she'll have more questions, and she'll come back to The Desk again."

"Maybe."

John smiled and began to unbutton his shirt, which hung loosely on his lanky frame. Half-way down, his fingers stopped and his jaw slackened. "I might not be there when she comes back."

Thogmartin guffawed midway through a crunch and fell back to the floor. His head made a loud thump. "Ow," he said between giggles.

"What?!"

Thogmartin rubbed his head, but continued to giggle. "At least Sjoerdsma will be happy. He can't get you to work a lick, and now you'll be volunteering for extra shifts."

"Shut up. Why do I even talk to you?"

"I wonder that all the—"

"She was really cute, you know." John finished unbuttoning his shirt and hung it beside his vest. "And always looking right at me. Dammit, you think she was waiting for me to say something?"

"Of course she was, she came to The Desk, didn't she?"

"No! You know what I mean." He pulled off his shoes and placed them side-by-side in his closet. "I mean, do you think she was *interested*. Like, she was waiting for me to make some conversation or something."

Thogmartin stretched his arms and let his legs flop to the floor. "I'll start calling you *Suave*aschen."

"Shut up." John stood and removed his pants. He folded them sharply on their creases and hung them beside his shirt and vest. He looked at Thogmartin. "She'll be back," he said.

"Yeah? Maybe *I*'ll be there."

John smirked. "Right."

Thogmartin sat up. "You're not the only one who works The Desk," he said.

"I'm the only one in this room who does."

"Won't be that way forever."

John turned back to his closet and began absently smoothing his vest again. "You think *you*—"

Thogmartin stood and glared at the back of John's head. "Yeah, I do. At least I—"

John laughed, but didn't turn around. "You're going to have to put in a few more hours practicing, I think," he said. "I mean, more than you already do."

Thogmartin's knuckles whitened, and then he relaxed his hands. "You're the exception, you know," he said quietly.

"Hmm?" said John. He examined the three retractable fountain pens he'd pulled out of his vest pocket.

"You, bouncing between the departments, working The Desk; you're the exception. Me, studying, practicing every day. That's where they expect me to be. Maybe even ahead of where they expect me to be."

John smiled and replaced the pens in his vest. "It's pretty tough being me."

"You know, John, there's one thing in particular that gives me great comfort, living here with you—"

"Oh yeah?"

"The knowledge that I'll always be able to kick your ass," he said.

John spun around. "At what?!" he said.

Thogmartin drew himself up to his full width, easily half-again wider than John's taller but bony form.

"Ah, I see," said John. "You meant literally. Thogmartin, you missed your calling. It's a cruel twist of fate that you weren't born into the Speakers."

They stared at each other for a moment before Thogmartin relaxed and laughed. He sang:

> *The president of the Brewer's Guild,*
> *With great determination,*
> *Made a beer that was the slickest*
> *Of all Social Lubrication.*

John laughed and joined Thogmartin:

> *Even from the mutest lips,*
> *That ale could wrest a story.*
> *Because of this peerless beer*
> *The Brewer rose to glory.*
>
> *And then one day a shadow*
> *Darkened his gleaming station:*
> *A brute of a man, dressed all in black,*
> *A Speaker for nineteen generations.*
>
> *He took a great swig of drink*
> *And his tongue began to wiggle.*
> *A flash, a crash, the bar was trashed*
> *And the brute let out a giggle.*
>
> *Enter Billy, the Brewer's son,*
> *To investigate the disturbance.*
> *Broken bottles, o'erturned mugs,*
> *He took it all in at a glance.*
>
> *Now,*

Little Billy, the Brewer's son,
Was born with blood of mead.
There wasn't a freer tongue you'd
Find in all the world, indeed.

Though it hurt deep in his heart
To hear the wounded patrons wail,
He'd never forgive the man in black
For spilling all that golden ale.

Billy locked eyes with the giggling galoot
And picked his way through the rubble.
Suddenly, his papa's place shown
Starkly white as Billy began to babble.

What Billy did in that blinding light
Not a man among them bore witness,
But once the stars were blinked away
The man in black lay Speechless.

John lay down on his bed and stared up at the ceiling. "Should I start calling you Billy, the Brewer's son, then?" he said.

"Maybe it'd stick."

John glanced at Thogmartin.

"You try carrying around a name like 'Thogmartin' for a while," he said. He sat on his bed, then laid back, ignoring the shirt and slacks trapped under him. "Billy, the Brewer's son, seems like something of an improvement."

They both stared up at the ceiling in silence for a moment.

"You don't suppose the Speakers sing songs about Archiving," said John.

"A daring tale of high-risk Archival: a lone Speaker, armed with only a lump of charcoal to make notes, facing a roomful of Multis, mouths foaming, vests gleaming, fountain-pens at the ready."

"It would make an amusing song, but I see your point."

"What are you going to tell Sjoerdsma?" said Thogmartin.

"That I've found my true calling. Up until now, nothing has seemed like a challenge. But The Desk has opened my eyes to the sort of excitement and job satisfaction available to the focused Multi. Nothing warms one's heart quite the way that seeing the look of satisfaction on the face of a happy customer does."

Thogmartin laughed. "He's going to see right through you, you know?" he said.

"Not likely."

Thogmartin laughed harder.

"Ok, fairly likely. But as long as I show up…" John shrugged.

"Remind me to kick your ass in the morning," Thogmartin said, yawning.

"Any particular reason?"

"Just 'cause you're you," he said.

Chapter 3

Lumin awoke when he heard his bedroom door open. He turned his head toward the door and saw his mother enter. She smiled at him, and he smiled weakly back at her.

He felt a dull throbbing in the back of his mind as he tried to nudge away the grogginess of sleep. He was ill, and, although yesterday was just a jumble of images and emotions in his head, he was certain this aching behind his eyes was a considerable improvement. When had he come here, to his old room? And why was his mother looking after him, and not—

"Feeling any better, sweetheart?" said Candesce. She sat on the edge of his bed and looked down at him.

"I think I must be," he said.

"You aren't sure?"

"Yesterday is a little vague." He sat up, wincing slightly when the pain in his head protested. He pushed the pain out of his way, and smiled at his mother.

"I'm glad you're feeling better, dear," she said and squeezed his knee through the blankets. "I told you a little rest would make all the difference. And now we'll put some food in you. No arguments." She cocked an eyebrow.

Lumin grinned. "Alright, alright," he said.

Candesce put her hands on her knees in preparation to stand.

"I dreamed about my first day of work last night. Yesterday? Well, sometime, anyway."

"Oh?" said Candesce. She relaxed back onto the bed, supporting herself with one hand.

"Yeah. That's really something, isn't it?" he said.

"Tell me about it," said Candesce.

"I was making my first ever patrol around the grounds of the junkyard when I stumbled across a girl. A girl!" He laughed and shook his head. "When was the last time I thought of my wife as a girl. My brains are still all scrambled." He closed his eyes and missed the look of confusion on his mother's face. "Anyway, I rushed in to save her from these towers of falling metal. Only I mostly just made a fool of myself."

Candesce laughed. "Sounds like quite the dream. Your first assignment for our House, with a bit of romance, too," she said. "The junkyard, huh?"

"Yeah."

"Not Oligarch's security? I thought nothing could be too prestigious for you."

Lumin scratched the back of his head. "Yeah, I guess I was kind of a brat about that back in the day."

Candesce chuckled. "To be so young that yesterday seems like a lifetime ago."

Incomprehension flickered across Lumin's face, but he chuckled, too. "Of course," he continued, "what eighteen-year-old kid doesn't think they have it all figured out. That, if only given the chance, he'd catapult his House above all others. When, really, 'duty' and 'responsibility' are just words he's heard. He can't understand them until he's lived them, when it's really mattered. No, I wouldn't change a moment of any of that now." He shook his head. "And there I went rambling. 'Wildly off on a tangent,' as my students always tell me."

Candesce gave him a bemused smile. "You're positively loopy this morning, sweetheart. Come on," she said as she stood, "let's get some food in you before you declare yourself Oligarch of New Dirkferdorn."

Lumin furrowed his brow at the back of his mother's head as she left the room. He hobbled out of bed and down the hall to the kitchen, still feeling slightly out of place in his body. A familiar voice Spoke far in the back of his mind, but his attention wandered at the sight of his mother setting a skillet on the stovetop.

He squinted out the row of brightly lit windows along the back wall, and as his eyes adjusted to the light, he resolved the garden beyond. He shuffled over to the kitchen table and sat.

"Garden's gotten a little out of hand," he said to himself.

"Hmm?" said Candesce, glancing over at him. Lumin continued to stare out the window, so Candesce went back to cracking eggs into the skillet. She started to absent-mindedly sing the Local Gossip:

The Civils out spanning the river
Called out to the 'garchy's fund-giver:

The bright morning light streaming into the kitchen, the over-grown garden out in the yard, the smell of fresh eggs frying all felt strangely familiar to Lumin.

Hey toss us some trey.
But he said 'no way.'
And now they may never deliver.

This was so typical of his childhood, he thought, but that wasn't it. "I dreamed this, too," he mumbled.

The Local Gossip pulled him out of his reverie. His mother, focusing as she was on scrambling the eggs in the skillet, was singing whichever verse popped into her head. The result was a jumble of news, much clearly ancient, punctuated with humming when some task of cooking required her concentration.

Lumin leaned back in his chair and let his mind go blank until Candesce slid his breakfast in front of him. He looked up and smiled back at her before lifting a forkful of eggs to his mouth. With the first swallow, he realized he'd been starving.

"Scrambled seemed appropriate this morning," she said and sat opposite Lumin.

Half-way through the plate of breakfast, Lumin paused. "I dreamed about Dad, too," he said.

"At the junkyard?"

"No," he said. "Here, just eating breakfast." He turned back to his food.

Candesce laughed. "You didn't dream that, sweetheart."

"Hmm?"

"That was yesterday morning."

"What?" Lumin looked at his mother.

"Yesterday morning. You wandered out here and collapsed. Gave your father and me quite a fright." Candesce leaned forward, seeing the panic creep onto Lumin's face. "Honey?"

"No," he said, sliding back in his chair. "Dad's dead. He's been dead five years."

"What are you talking about?" She reached out and touched his forehead with the palm of her hand.

Lumin's breathing quickened and the color drained out of his face. He felt the dull ache in his head begin to move forward as his control slipped. And the voice, calling from somewhere far off, Spoke to him again.

"Your dad's fine," said Candesce. "He's at work. He'll be home tonight."

Lumin shook his head and tried to stand. He stumbled and found himself down on one knee, his mother squatting in front of him and gripping him firmly by the shoulders.

"It's alright, sweetheart," said Candesce. "Let's get you back to bed."

Chapter 4

Jim Sjoerdsma combed through his thinning hair with his fingers as he walked down the hall to his office. The soft tinkling of metal cards on his vest and the whirring of the auto-winder in the card reader strapped to his left thigh were barely audible over the hissing of the pneumatics in the wall beside him. As he approached his office, the sound of music from a practice organ grew louder.

He rounded the last corner and saw that his door stood ajar, the music clearly coming from within his office. He stepped up to his door and leaned against the frame.

Inside, John Sevaschen coaxed a slow and haunting fugue from the little organ. He pumped the organ steadily with his left foot whilst his long thin fingers walked and leapt across the keyboard, showing a grace and poise foreign to his lanky body in any other context.

Sjoerdsma listened in silence for a moment. "That's from the Inter-City Championship last year, isn't it?"

"That's right," said John as he continued to play.

"An excellent match, as I remember it. I especially liked your subject."

"It was an inspired theme. One of my favorites," said John. "And an excellent choice for the competition, if I do say so myself."

"Mmm," said Sjoerdsma.

"It's slow and deliberate, see," said John as the theme made a redundant entry, stating itself once again in its original fullness. "Which gave my opponent a fair amount of confidence when he developed his answer." John answered the theme with his left hand, first in an abridged re-statement of the theme, then arpegiatted and in double time.

"It has a very nice effect," said Sjoerdsma.

"I thought so, as did the judges. And then here," said John, as he played a brief turn in the high register, "he brought in this delightful counter-subject. The judges penalized him, of course, because instead of developing it, he simply repeated it a few times. They probably thought he was struggling, and maybe they were right. But I find the effect very pleasant nonetheless." The first counter-subject dropped away, and John introduced another, which was closely mimicked by the following voice. "And then here," he said, leaning lower over the keyboard and striking the keys with a new intensity, "this was really inspired. He pushed into the major key. Brilliant."

"Yes," said Sjoerdsma.

John answered in the minor key, where the piece remained. "Such a pity that he caved under the pressure. I nudged him back to minor and his subject was lost: false stretto." John sighed and stopped playing. He spun around on the bench. "Hardly worth bothering after that. Nothing interesting to speak of, and the scores reflected that."

"It was an inspired match, John. Really something. You should use that theme again sometime, see what comes of it."

John smiled. "I may do that. Of course, the acoustics in here," he gestured vaguely, "hardly do it justice. Maybe if you actually threw out some of this—"

"How was working The Desk yesterday?" Sjoerdsma moved into the room and settled into a chair beside the organ with a high, worn wooden back and a faded cushion. He nudged aside a stack of sheet music with his foot, one of many that cluttered the floor and the top of the little organ.

John contorted his face into a toothy, false grin. "Perfect. Wonderful! Everything I'd hoped it could be. It's given me focus and determination. You'll never have to worry about me again, sir."

"Is that right?" Sjoerdsma leaned back in his chair and squinted suspiciously at John.

"Absolutely, sir." John strained to smile wider.

"And you wouldn't object to taking a few more shifts there, then?"

"I'd be thrilled, sir. As many shifts as you can give me."

Sjoerdsma sucked on his tongue for a moment, then abandoned that to chew on his lip. His gaze stayed fixed to John's taught grin. "You have an interesting history here, John, and I probably don't have to remind you of that. But you may find this informative, so let's go over it, hmm?"

John blinked but held his smile.

"The first time I dragged you away from your practice organ, I set you to work in Retrieval. It wasn't a very glamorous position, but nonetheless remarkable for a Multi of your age. And yet, if I recall correctly, you didn't hesitate to tell me just how unglamorous you thought it was. An opinion I was forced to take seriously when you decided your attendance was no longer mandatory."

Sjoerdsma looked up at the ceiling for a moment, then back at John. "I believe next was Archival: an extremely important job, and positively unheard of for a boy your age. Not challenging enough, you said. So then I put you on Field Archival. I thought that might peak your interest. But I was rewarded with complaints from both you *and* your superiors." Sjoerdsma sighed.

"This is—" said John.

"Wait for it, son," said Sjoerdsma. "Ah, yes, next was that teaching fiasco, training those first and second year apprentices. Highly irregular for one so fresh out of training himself." He scratched the back of his head. "Well, at least you showed up everyday for that one. Pity that you spent a great deal more time showing off and playing the organ than you did instructing your pupils.

"And so I pulled out all the stops for you, John. I called in every favor ever owed to me, and I've got you on The Desk. There's not a more challenging or prestigious job in this guild, though dealing with you arguably presents an equal challenge."

"Thank you, sir," said John.

"John, I've known you for about eight years now, so I think I know you pretty well. And while you are a singular student, I've also had a great many students over the years. And I'll say this: you were not thrilled by your job at The Desk."

"Oh, no, I assure you, sir, it was everything—"

"But," said Sjoerdsma, waving his hands as though to physically push aside John's protest. "But, something obviously did happen yesterday which has changed your outlook. I wish it had been the work, but what, if not that, could it have been, hmm?"

John opened his mouth to respond, but Sjoerdsma held up his hand.

"There are only two things that I think would have this effect on you," said Sjoerdsma. He cradled his jaw in his hand. "The first would be some kind of challenge. A dare. A bet. And the other? Well, that would be a girl."

John blushed.

"Aha. And was she a Multi or a customer?"

John mumbled something and Sjoerdsma leaned forward. John cleared his throat. "She was a customer, sir."

Sjoerdsma sighed. He leaned back in the chair again and his shoulders sagged. "Well, I suppose if it gets you to work every day."

"Don't worry, sir. I won't let you down."

"No, John, you won't. I'd tell you that was a threat if I thought it'd make any difference." He stood up. "Go, get out of here," he said.

"Thank you, sir," said John as he moved to the door.

"And John, do try to focus on the work. Try to enjoy it. It is why you're there."

"Yes, sir," he said and ducked out the door.

Chapter 5

Ardent craned his neck around the front door and peered into the empty living room beyond. "Hello, hello," he said and his voice echoed off the hardwood floors, hardly dampened by the sparsely furnished room.

The sound of bare feet padding on the polished floor preceded Candesce into the living room. "Come in, Ardent, dear," she said and smiled tiredly. She continued toward her spindly, wooden chair—its comfort disguised by its simplicity—as Ardent ducked around the door.

He kissed Candesce's cheek. "I've come to tease my little cousin," he said as Candesce eased herself into the chair.

"Ordinarily, I'd encourage you, but Lumin's sick in bed."

"Well, I'll be damned," he said. "Who knew he was human just like the rest of us?"

"I'd always suspected he just might be."

Ardent sat opposite her in one of the handful of chairs in the otherwise unadorned room. "It's nothing serious?"

"Oh, no. I think half of it's just stress."

"Well, then we needn't worry."

"It's a mother's prerogative," she said. She leaned back in the chair and closed her eyes. "Your big day just passed, did it? Come to lord it over Lumin."

"Absolutely."

She laughed. "Is the real world everything you'd hoped it would be? Looking forward to that first paycheck, I'd bet."

Ardent sighed and put his head in his hands theatrically. "I think my mother expects me to," his chair creaked, "to start," he breathed in sharply, "doing my own laundry."

"Oh, how the mighty have fallen," she said. "How is it, working for Fulgor?"

"I hold onto the hope that one day I shall do something right."

"It's only your first week. And he's only known you for eighteen years. You just have to give him some time." She smiled.

"Everyone told stories about him, you know. They couldn't be true, of course, because they were far too horrible. Now I realize that everyone was trying to be polite, in case he heard. And trust me, he hears everything." He glanced around the room suspiciously.

Candesce laughed. "You'll settle in. And he'll get used to having you around," she said. "Everything will seem normal and comfortable, and then you'll get married."

Ardent blanched. "One step at a time. Please. I'm happy not to think about that for a while yet."

Candesce laughed.

"Besides," he said, "I'd like the chance to distinguish myself a little. So I'll get a good match."

"I really don't think you need to worry."

"But you think Lumin's worried."

"Hmm?"

He shifted in his chair. "You said he was stressed—"

"Oh. Well, everyone is expecting so much from him, and he puts so much pressure on himself."

"That doesn't sound like the Lumin I know."

Candesce smiled and put her finger to her lips. "Don't tell anyone, but he's really not so different from the rest of us. Besides, you keep him honest."

"Me? I can barely keep up—"

"You're always one step behind him." She reached out and squeezed his knee. "I don't envy you that position. It can't be easy. But you there, nudging him forward, that's a gift no one else has given him."

"I— I don't know what to say."

Candesce smiled, but after a moment her expression became pensive and she looked away. "It's very nearly time for Lambent and me to meet with Elder Scintilla to discuss Lumin's first assignment. Ardent, I wonder if—" She looked him in the eye. "I wonder if I might have your counsel."

"What? I couldn't begin to— well, I mean, whatever you need, of course."

"It's just that, well, you know a young man Lumin's age doesn't tell his mother everything."

Ardent nodded.

"And earlier today," Candesce continued, "he told me he'd had this dream. And in it, his first assignment was as security at the junkyard."

Ardent chuckled. "Lumin?"

"My thoughts precisely," said Candesce earnestly. "But this dream must have been quite vivid." She squeezed the armrest of her chair, and then shook her head. "I couldn't entirely follow what he was talking about, but he had real conviction about it. He was so certain that this position was exactly where he needed to be."

Ardent leaned back in his chair and looked up at the ceiling. "That's quite a reversal. And now how will I make him jealous, if all he wants is the junkyard?"

"So he hasn't mentioned anything like that to you before?"

Ardent shook his head. "I thought he was expecting something extraordinary." Ardent sat up a bit straighter and hastened to add, "Although I'm sure he would do an exceptional job with whatever position Elder Scintilla chose for him."

"Of course, dear. But he'd grumble about it in your ear," she said with a smile. She stood and Ardent followed suit. "Lumin will feel better in a few days, and then I expect you to come by and give him a hard time, hmm? And listen to him. If there's something that we need to know..."

"You can count on me. I'll see you in a few days, then," he said.

Chapter 6

Lumin entered the shack that served as Mr. Baldwin's office. If it weren't for the large, painted metal sign outside clearly labeling this as the 'Office,' and the fact that Lumin had already been here once before today, he might have totally overlooked the building. It wasn't very large and blended in with the surroundings, as it appeared to be constructed entirely of salvaged materials. The slightly mangled screen door clanged shut behind Lumin. The piston that should have slowed it obviously had not faired as well as the door itself.

Mr. Baldwin, a short, round man, sat behind a large desk, duplicating inventory tables in preparation for Archival. He looked up at Lumin, tossed his pen aside, and leaned back in his chair. He took a sip from a chipped coffee mug, managing to add a stain to the faded and sometimes torn shirt he wore. Lumin felt a certain comfort that all this fit with his prejudices about the junkyard.

Mr. Baldwin gave Lumin an appraising look. "Well, what happened, kid?" he said.

"Sir?"

"This is a simple gig for your type, kid. And I'm looking at you and something happened. So spill it."

"I met the girl you mentioned," said Lumin.

"And?"

"And I saved her from some falling metal."

Mr. Baldwin's eyes widened. "She ok?" he said.

"She's fine, sir," said Lumin.

Mr. Baldwin slid his mug onto the desk. He squinted at Lumin. "Not like Caprice to need saving, kid."

Lumin swallowed.

Mr. Baldwin drummed his fingers on his desk and studied Lumin's face for a moment. "You just be sure you're not getting in her way," he said. He looked away from Lumin and reached for his mug.

"Is she your apprentice?" said Lumin.

"Caprice?" Mr. Baldwin came dangerously close to spilling his coffee. "You think I'd take her on as apprentice?"

Lumin smiled. "She did seem a little out of place," he said.

Mr. Baldwin stood and leaned across his desk. He gravely looked Lumin in the eye. "I've seen your type before, kid. You just took your first step out into the world, and you already think you know everything. And they told me you were clever. Should have guessed that'd make it worse."

"I don't understand—"

"That's right," said Mr. Baldwin. He sat back in his chair and looked blankly at the wall. "That girl is the most important thing going on 'round here, and I don't want you getting in her way."

"Then why isn't she—"

"My apprentice? I don't know what 'clever' means to you people," Mr. Baldwin looked back at Lumin, "you *Speakers*. But that girl brings new meaning to the word. If you think I'd wish this," he gestured at his office, "on her, then maybe you shouldn't come back tomorrow. No, you do your job. You stay out of her way. You do a little *listening*, and maybe you learn something. Now get out of here."

Lumin opened his mouth. "Yes, sir," he said. He walked back out into the bright sunlight. The door clanged shut behind him.

Lumin startled awake. His room was bright with afternoon light bouncing off the neighboring house. He stared up at the layered hardwood beam that stretched across his ceiling.

Chapter 7

The current evolution of The Desk stretched no less than half a city-block wide, a towering monument of gray stone, elevated and recessed from the street by twenty wide steps. The high, ornamented roof-line jutted out imposingly over the granite plateau that prefaced the windows of The Desk, keeping the space shaded for the bulk of the day. Thrust into the wall, stacked two high but staggered, were the windows. A Multi manned each of the lower windows, with an occasional attendant in an upper window to assist with especially complex requests. Without exception, where a Multi occupied the upper window, the customer stood before it, flanked by the lower windows, and attended by all three occupants.

As much as the architects had designed The Desk to awe its customers, they also meant it to be efficient. Nowhere was this more obvious than within. Despite the impressive, dark, hardwood desks and chairs, polished from use, and the gleaming brass piping stretching up the walls to the ceiling that comprised the ventilation and pneumatics, the room seemed surprisingly narrow and cramped. This hadn't always been the case, but refinements to the design over the decades had pushed the rear wall, now padded, closer and closer to the Multi's stations, with the result that, in spite of the bustling of activity, the milling of the crowd and the hissing of the pneumatics, the customer could be heard even at a whisper.

"It's a classic," shouted the thin, old man standing in front of John. He brought his head in closer to the window, leaning on his cane. "They don't make 'em like this anymore, the fools."

"And that's the problem, is it?" said John. Meanwhile, his left hand danced across the cards on the right side of his vest, like a fiddler finding a note on the neck of his instrument. He looked over the man's shoulder, scanning the crowd, as he pulled a card off his vest and clicked it into the reader on his left thigh.

"Damned straight, that's the problem," shouted the man.

John absent-mindedly tapped his left foot as the Twelve-points on the touch pad of his reader began to jab at the meat of his first two fingers.

"These kids these days won't even look at ya unless ya've got a Rhueling model, with all its stamped parts," shouted the man.

John pulled out a Requisition sheet, and clicked open his fountain pen.

"Junk," shouted the man. "Cheap junk."

John's gaze drifted over the man's other shoulder and continued to dance from face to face. "But not the Gibson, eh?" he said. He scrawled, beneath the serial number printed in Twelve-points on the Requisition sheet, 'Gibson 6500 Schematics' and the Vesting number as it was listed on his data card.

"No, not the Gibson," shouted the man. "The Gibson is a work of art."

As John rolled the Requisition form into it's capsule and launched it through the pneumatic, his gaze strayed down the street.

"Boy!" shouted the man. "I'm standing right here."

John instinctively ducked as the handle of the man's cane floated within an inch of his face. Their eyes met.

"Of course you are, sir," said John. "And you were telling me about the Gibson."

"I haven't forgotten why I'm here, boy," the man shouted. He leaned on his cane again.

The two stared at each other for a moment. John ejected the data card and returned it to his vest.

The man's face softened. "Every piece of the Gibson is hand made," he shouted. "Hand fitted. No slop to be found in the entire engine. Not like this new crap they're turning out. And they won't even fix 'em anymore, can you believe it?"

A capsule arrived in the pneumatic with a thud.

"Said I was on my own to get the new part made," shouted the man. "Kid says, if I get the part, he'll fix my Gibson, but I'm on my own for the part. Can you believe it?"

John extracted the schematics from the capsule and unrolled them on his desk. "Are these the correct schematics, sir?" said John.

The old man leaned his head in the window and peered at the plans. "Yeah, that's my baby," he shouted.

"Excellent, Mr.—"

"Althrop Gherrig," shouted the man.

John wrote the name on a form that had come packed with the schematics. "In two weeks, the schematics are due back in the Archive, Mr. Gherrig. If you do not return them by that time, they will be collected—"

"I've been here before, boy," shouted the man. He snatched up the tethered pen on the edge of John's desk and signed the form.

John handed the man the schematics, and he hobbled away down the steps. John began to scan the crowd again as he sent the Release form back through the pneumatic. A figure moved in front of John's window. "How can I help you today?" said John, before turning to see who was before him.

"Well," said a young, blond man not much older than John, "I heard something today, and I've succumbed to my curiosity."

"You've come to the right place," said John.

"Yeah. Uh, do you have anything on a boiler-less steam engine?" The man blushed.

John scribbled 'anything on boiler-less steam engine' on the Requisition form. "That sounds very interesting," he said. His left foot stopped its thoughtless tapping and he frowned for an instant, then he added a very truncated Vesting number to the form. He sent it off in the pneumatic.

The man scratched the back of his head and looked at the ground. "Well, it's just a rumor I heard."

John smiled. "Sounds like something out of the Local Gossip, you know?"

The man flushed redder. "Yeah, uh, well, I did first hear about it in a Local Gossip," he said.

"I don't think you can put too much stock in those things," said John.

"Oh, I know. I just heard someone down south was working on it."

"You mean, outside the city?"

"Yeah, I think so," said the man. He dipped his head still lower.

"I bet someone's just putting you on. One of those minstrels thought it sounded clever and he's just messing with you," said John. A capsule thunked to a stop, and John pulled it out. "Yeah," he said, "there's nothing about it in the Archive."

"Then you must be right," said the man. He laughed nervously. "It's just some joke. Thanks anyway." He tried to disappear into the crowd.

John looked down at the slip that read 'Not in Archive.' "Huh," he said. A bell chimed and he looked at his watch. He gave one last, quick glance to the crowd, then sighed and lowered the cover on his window.

Chapter 8

Caprice carefully lowered the gear into its place in the wrist watch with a tiny pair of tweezers in her right hand. Her pinky and ring fingers rested on her left hand, which surrounded the partially assembled watch and held it firmly in place on the desk. Scattered around the desk were a number of other small parts, springs and gears. Up near the wall sat the watch face, hands and crystal beside a very tiny crowbar. The gear dropped into place, meshing with its neighbors.

As she glanced up to locate the next gear she needed, some khaki-colored motion caught her eye. Reflected in the mirror on her desk, she saw her father standing in the doorway, wearing his customary (and perpetually grease smudged) coveralls, and with his arms behind his back. He smiled.

"Hi, Daddy," she said, turning around.

"Hey baby girl," he said. He waddled into the room a little awkwardly. Caprice stood on her tip-toes and kissed him on the cheek.

"How was work?" she said.

"Another day, another cog," he said. He looked over her shoulder. "Are you fixing another one? Don't you have enough of those?"

Caprice grinned and looked away from her father as she twisted one of the three watches on her left arm. "After I fixed the second one, I couldn't tell you what time it was anymore." She dropped her arms to her sides and a fourth watch, this on her right arm, slid down to her wrist. She looked back at her father's face. "Now I have to keep fixing more of them so I can get a more accurate average."

"Is that right?" he said.

She cocked her eyebrow mischievously. "Whatcha got there?" she said.

"I brought you something."

"Really?" She leaned around her father trying to get a peek.

He laughed and brought a half assembled collection of metal parts out from behind his back. He handed it to Caprice.

"Ooh, that's heavy," she said, swaying theatrically under the weight.

"Yeah," he said and laughed. He leaned in and pointed to a pinion gear. "They've got me making these this week."

Caprice looked closely at the gear, her eye's occasionally flicking back to her father's face. "Looks good, daddy," she said. She smiled broadly.

Her father blushed and scratched the back of his head.

"So, uh, what is it?" she said.

"It's a coffee grinder," he said.

She looked back down at the apparatus, turning it side to side. "You're teasing me," she said.

"No, honest."

"But it's got too many parts," she said.

"Well, it's got a lot of parts, yeah, but it's special, see," he said. "You're supposed to wind it up, like, and then when you want to grind your coffee, you just flip a switch."

Caprice fiddled with a large fly-wheel on the grinder. "I guess I see," she said. "Seems pretty silly, doesn't it?"

"Yeah, it'd probably just break down all the time. Anyway, I saw this one just lying around. See, quality control tossed it, or something, so I thought—" He frowned. "I dunno what I thought. Hell, it's just a piece of junk. You don't want this thing. I don't know what I was thinking—" He reached for the grinder.

"Daddy," she said, "thanks for bringing it for me."

"Yeah," he said. His arms dropped and his shoulders slumped. "Yeah, alright."

Caprice hefted the grinder up to eye level. "I'll take it apart, figure out what's wrong with it." She looked over the top of the grinder at her father.

"You don't have to do that."

"It'll be fun." She grinned. "You just try and stop me."

Her father smiled weakly back at her.

"Vishton!" said a woman's voice.

Her father cringed.

"Momma?" said Caprice.

Vishton nodded.

Caprice's mother appeared at the door. "Vishton," she said.

He turned around to face her.

She was still dressed in her work clothes, minus her apron. The white blouse, with its green and gold patch at the shoulder, was stained in a pattern that marked out where the apron had been.

"I was calling for you. The least you could do—"

Caprice stepped out from behind her father.

Her mother caught sight of the partially assembled grinder in Caprice's hands.

"Oh not again," said her mother. "More junk. You keep bringing this trash home!" She waved her arm at the grinder. "And someone is going to see you taking it and throw you out on your ass. Then where will we be?"

"No one cares, dear," said Vishton. "They were throwing it out—"

"And you had to bring it home. You don't think they were throwing it out for a *reason*?"

"How was work today, Momma?" said Caprice.

"It was *work*, not that I expect *you* to understand what that means," said her mother. "Everyone else your age has an apprenticeship, but—"

"I won't have her taking some dead-end apprenticeship," said her father.

"You won't, hmm? How can you keep filling her head with these dreams we'll never be able to afford? Start living in the real world."

"I know plenty about the real world," said Vishton.

"Then you know damn well that she should be bringing home a paycheck."

Caprice turned back to her desk and set the grinder down in the one empty space she could find. She leaned down and examined a small, engraved, metal plaque at the base of the grinder casing. It read, "Coffee Auto-Grinder CAG1." She slid her finger slowly over it. She settled back into her chair and skimmed over the array of watch parts. She picked up her tweezers and selected a small gear. Balancing her right hand on her left, she began to lower it into place.